CONTENTS

1

MOVIE MAKERS

Wren House leaned her ten-speed against the side of the small, white house. She flipped back her long brown hair and grinned as Tim Avery dropped his bike onto the lawn in front of Amos Pike's house. Two minutes later Bess Talbot pedaled up beside them. She was always slow. She didn't want the wind to mess up her blonde hair just in case Wren's brother Neil saw her.

"I'll knock," said Tim. He carried the camcorder for their special school project at Jordan Christian Academy.

Wren lifted the colorful bouquet of zinnias and dahlias out of the basket behind her bike seat and ran to the door to wait with Tim.

Bess tucked her pink blouse into her jeans. She already looked neat and tidy, but she wanted to make double sure she did.

"I think I should get to knock," Bess said.

"Why?" asked Wren.

"You got to bring the flowers and Tim got to carry the

camera. I should get to do something." Bess reached around Tim and knocked a gentle little tap with the very tips of her knuckles.

"I don't think Mr. Pike heard that," said Tim. He pounded on the door with the side of his fist.

"Well, everybody on Green Street heard that," said Wren.

Tim grinned. "Do you think so?" He hiked up his faded jeans. "I'm excited about making a movie with Amos Pike. He'll be great."

Wren nodded. The three ten year olds stood impatiently shifting from one foot to another. A pickup rattled past. Two boys shouted at each other three houses down.

"Why isn't he answering?" asked Bess. She rubbed her knuckles as if she'd hurt herself when she knocked.

"I wonder if something happened to Mr. Pike," said Wren.

Bess frowned at Wren. "Don't you dare make a mystery out of this! You know your mom told you to let your dad do the detective work since he's the detective in the family. You always want to make a mystery out of everything, and you always get in trouble.

"Not always," said Wren, but she knew that only once had she really found a mystery.

"I love to solve mysteries," said Tim. He and Wren had become friends because they both liked to do detective work. "We did a good job solving the Wheeler mystery,

The Search for
THE MISSING
NEIGHBOR

HILDA STAHL

Accent Books™ is an imprint of David C. Cook Publishing Co.
David C. Cook Publishing Co., Elgin, Illinois 60120
David C. Cook Publishing Co., Weston, Ontario
Nova Distribution Ltd., Newton Abbot, England

SEARCH FOR THE MISSING NEIGHBOR
©1986 by Word Spinners, Inc.
Revised 1992

Cover design and illustration by Terry Julien
First Printing, 1986
Printed in the United States of America
96 95 94 93 92 6 5 4 3 2

Library of Congress Catalog Card Number 85-73829

ISBN 0-78140-513-0

didn't we?" He grinned at Wren and his blue eyes danced. Once Wren had hated Tim and been embarrassed to be his friend, but no longer.

Suddenly a small, black dog tore around the house, barking and nipping at Tim's ragged tennis shoes and the worn bottoms of his jeans.

"Don't let him bite me!" cried Bess. She jumped behind Wren, not caring that she was almost a head taller than Wren. "Tim, don't let him bite me! Save me, Wren!"

"He's not after you, Bess." Wren tried to pull the dog away from Tim's foot, but she couldn't.

"Stop it, dog!" Tim pushed the camera into Wren's hands and grabbed for the dog's collar. The dog snarled and snapped, but Tim held the collar and kept the dog down. "Get Amos Pike, Wren!"

Wren's hands were full so she kicked the door. It popped open and Amos stood there, rubbing sleep from his eyes. But when he saw the dog, he woke up fast.

"Buster! Stop it!" Amos Pike picked up the dog, rubbing its neck and kissing its furry face. Then he put it in the house and shut the door. "I hope he didn't hurt you kids. Buster's a good watch dog. He's little, but he's mighty."

"I wasn't scared." Bess tossed her head and stepped from behind Wren.

"Does he always take such good care of you, Mr. Pike?" asked Wren.

Tim rubbed his ankle and retied his shoes. "He sure didn't want us here, Mr. Pike."

"Call me Amos. All my friends call me Amos." Amos Pike grinned and smoothed back his sparse gray hair. "Right now I don't have any friends. All of 'em are gone. Only Buster's left. Buster and I have been together for ten years and he goes everywhere with me. He takes good care of me and I try to do the same for him." He looked at the kids. "I didn't think you kids would be back."

Wren said, "We wanted to take a movie of you. Remember?"

"I didn't take you seriously since you didn't come the last three days."

"We couldn't get here," said Tim. He didn't want to say that it was because he'd been busy taking care of his mom. He didn't like people to know that she was an alcoholic and always drunk.

"I brought you some flowers," said Wren, thrusting out the bouquet that she'd picked from her own yard. "I remember you said you like flowers." She motioned to the straggly row of marigolds along the cracked sidewalk.

Amos took the flowers as he blinked tears from his bright blue eyes. He touched the petals. "I don't recall anyone ever bringing flowers to me. Thanks." He narrowed his eyes. "When you were here before, you asked me about my neighbor, but I don't rightly remember your names."

"I'm Tim Avery and I live not far from here on Bond

Street. We're doing a school assignment for our fifth grade class at Jordan Christian Academy."

Bess folded her hands in front of her and said, "I'm Bess Talbot and I live on Lyons Street. It's across town in a better neighborhood than this." Wren and Tim jabbed her and she looked at them and said, "What?"

"That's all right," said Amos. "I know this is a run-down neighborhood. But it's all I can afford. The house is mine, all paid for and everything. When I first bought it thirty years ago, this was a nice place to live. Me and my wife lived here until she passed on five years ago." He peered at Wren. "What'd you say your name was?"

Wren moved restlessly. She hated the reaction she always got when she told her name for the first time to a stranger. She squared her small shoulders and lifted her chin. She might as well get it over. "My name is Wren House."

Amos chuckled and shook his head. "What a name. Is that your real name or a phony name like famous actors give?"

Wren flushed. "It's my real name. My mom named me that so nobody would ever forget my name."

"I forgot it."

"I only told you my first name."

"Did you now? You should've told me all of it."

"Why is that?"

He chuckled. "I've been fretting for three days now

9

trying to recall your names. I wanted to give you a call and see if you really did mean to make a movie of me."

Wren knew he was lonely, but she hadn't realized that it meant so much to him to be in their movie for school. She was glad they had come. "We're ready to take the movie now if you're ready."

"Dressed like this?" Amos looked down at his worn pants and tattered flannel shirt.

"Do you have better clothes?" asked Bess.

Wren frowned at her, and Bess shrugged, looking hurt.

"We want you to look just the way you do every day," said Tim. He didn't see anything wrong with Amos Pike's clothes. Tim always wore old clothes. He took the camcorder from Wren and aimed it at Amos. "Why don't you work in your flower garden."

"Where is it?" asked Bess.

Wren nudged her again. Sometimes Wren wondered about Bess.

Amos bent down to take a tiny weed from beside a scraggly marigold. The marigolds stood about five inches tall and each blossom was about the size of a dime. "Does this look good?" He grinned up at Tim, showing his loose dentures.

"It's great," said Tim, hitting the record button. "Walk to your door now and let your dog out."

"Not the dog!" cried Bess, jumping behind Wren again.

"Buster won't hurt you with me here," said Amos with a chuckle. "Don't be afraid of him." Amos opened the door and Buster took one flying leap and landed in Amos's arms. The dog licked Amos's face, then leaped down and rolled over, played dead, begged, shook hands and jumped through the circle Amos made with his thin arms. Tim got it all on tape.

"This is good stuff," said Wren. "Probably better than what Paula Gantz did." Paula lived across the street from Wren and had been her enemy as long as Wren could remember. Just this year Paula had left public school to attend JCA, so it seemed like Wren had to put up with her twenty- four hours a day.

Just then a small brown car pulled up at the curb and a short woman in her fifties stepped out. "Amos!" she called angrily.

"Oh, no! Come on, Buster!" Amos grabbed Buster and ran into the house, slamming the door with a bang.

The woman marched right to the door and pounded on it, but Amos didn't appear. "You open this door right now, Amos Pike! I mean it!" She suddenly turned and spotted Tim with the camera pointed right at her. "Don't you dare take a picture of me."

"He's not," said Bess. "It's a camcorder for making movies."

"Movie!" shrieked the woman, throwing up her hands. "What has that old man done now?" She ran toward Tim.

"Don't you dare keep that camera going! I mean it, little boy. Stop that!"

"She wants you to stop, Tim," said Bess weakly.

Tim held the camera to his side. The woman hesitated, then rushed to her car and drove away. But as she did, Tim aimed the camcorder at the car.

"Did you get the license?" Wren's dark eyes sparkled as she danced around Tim.

"I got it," said Tim with a wide grin that stretched out his freckles.

Bess groaned and shook her head. "This had better not be another mystery, Wren. As your best friend I can only take so much."

Wren and Tim looked at each other and burst out laughing.

"I think it's a mystery," said Tim.

"I think it is, too," said Wren. She leaped into the air and kicked her heels.

2

AMOS PIKE

The door opened a tiny crack and Amos asked, "Is she gone?"

"She's gone," said Wren, hiding the grin on her face.

"She got mad when she saw me with the camcorder," said Tim.

Chuckling, Amos pulled the door open. Buster stood at his feet. "Stella's always mad. Come in, kids. She might come back."

Bess tugged on Wren's t-shirt. "Isn't it time to go home?"

Wren pulled free and followed Tim into the house. Bess tagged after them.

Amos shook his head and his blue eyes twinkled. "That Stella doesn't know when to quit."

"Who's Stella?" asked Tim. He held the camcorder to his eye and pointed it at Amos.

"Sit down and I'll tell you," said Amos, slapping his leg as if he knew a funny joke. He walked to the table to arrange Wren's flowers in a tall clear vase. He touched the petals and smiled again.

Wren glanced around the clean, tidy front room. Amos was a good housekeeper. She could tell he liked to read. One wall was covered with shelves of books, dozens of magazines were stacked in another case beside a portable TV, and a newspaper was open on the coffee table in front of the couch. One chair was covered with a faded red towel. Buster jumped into the chair and curled up, keeping one sleepy eye on Amos.

Bess walked to the couch and sat on the edge with her hands folded in her lap.

Tim held the camcorder to his eye and Wren watched as Tim followed Amos from place to place. Finally Tim laid the camcorder on the dining room table. "That should do it," he said.

"Now tell us about that woman," said Wren. She just knew that something exciting was going to happened.

Amos sat in his chair with a loud sigh. He leaned forward and slammed his fist into his palm. "Do you know how mad she makes me? All the time, nag, nag, nag." He mimicked the woman. "Amos, why don't you let me come stay with you and take care of your house for you? Amos, you're too old to live alone. I'm your sister, Amos, and I want to take care of you." He threw up his hands and Buster lifted his head and barked. "She just wants free room and board. She never cared for me while her husband was alive and taking care of her. But now that

14

she's alone and has lost her place, she wants to move in here with me. Well, I won't have her here. She'd kick Buster out and then where would I be? She hates Buster with a passion."

"Did he bite her?" asked Bess anxiously.

"Twice," said Amos. He patted Buster as a reward.

Bess shivered.

"Why don't you just tell her to stay away," said Wren.

"I have. Now, she says she's going to put me away in one of them nursing homes."

"Can she do that?" asked Tim.

"She thinks she can. But I won't let her. No siree. I won't let her and Buster here won't either. Will you, Buster, my boy?"

Buster shook his head and Wren laughed.

"Is there any way we can help you?" asked Wren.

"I don't think so. God is always with me and He helps me." Amos smiled from one to the other. "But if I can think of anything, I'll let you know."

Tim's face lit up with an idea. "Amos, will you come to school next week and meet all the fifth grade?"

"Do you really want me?" asked Amos.

"We're going to show the movies we made and the teacher is going to grade them," said Wren. "The movies will be shown next Wednesday. Please come."

Amos slapped his knee and laughed. "Nothing will keep me away. Nothing!"

"Don't bring Buster, though," said Bess.

Wren frowned at Bess, then turned back to Amos. "I think you should bring him. I'll get special permission from Miss Brewster."

"You kids have brought a lot of sunshine to my life, and I won't forget it. No, I won't." He pushed himself up. "Do you kids want a cookie? I baked a batch three days ago for you and put them in the freezer since you didn't come."

"Thank you," said Tim. "I'd like one."

"Me, too," said Wren.

"What kind are they?" asked Bess.

"Chocolate drop. My wife's specialty. She taught me how to bake them years ago." Amos led them to the kitchen where he opened a small freezer in one corner of the room. Tim was right behind him with the camera. Amos lifted out a plate wrapped in foil and set it in the middle of the small kitchen table. "Want tea or milk?"

"I can't drink tea," said Bess. "My mother doesn't want me to drink it until I'm older."

"Water will be fine," said Wren. She didn't know if Amos could afford to give them each a glass of milk.

Several minutes later they said good-bye with a promise to visit again soon, and rode away. A block from Amos's house Wren turned and spotted a familiar car. "Tim! Stop!" Tim turned and together they rode back to Bess.

"What's wrong?" asked Bess.

16

"I saw Stella's car!" Wren's cheeks were bright red and her eyes sparkled with excitement. "See?" She pointed to a small brown car parked at the curb. There was no one in it.

Tim nodded. "It's her car all right. I bet she's going to sneak up on Amos and try to get inside his house."

"Let's ride back and see." Wren led the way, the wind whipping her hair back. She felt as if she were flying to the rescue of a client the way her dad did. In a few minutes she stopped across the street from Amos's house. Her heart raced. "Shh!" She held her finger to her lips, then pointed across the street. Stella was sneaking around the side of the house, trying the windows. They could hear Buster barking in a frenzy from inside.

"I'll stop her," Tim declared, riding across the street.

"I don't think I should be here," said Bess.

Wren followed Tim. He rode right up to Stella, with the camera.

"Did you lose something?" asked Wren.

Stella shrieked and covered her face with her purse.

"You kids get away from here," snapped Stella from behind her purse.

Wren pounded on the door. "Amos, we're back! Stella's back, too."

He opened the door a crack, winked at Wren, and shut it again.

Stella practically bounced up and down as she pointed

to the door with a trembling finger. Her round face was bright red. "See? See the way he is? He can't be trusted on his own. He's old and senile and just plain dumb!"

"He's our friend," said Wren.

"He doesn't have friends," snapped Stella.

"He does now," said Bess, who had followed the others. Wren felt like cheering.

"We'll see about this!" Stella marched off, swinging her purse at her side. Her heels tap-tapped angrily on the cracked sidewalk. Tim followed silently after her, the camera catching it all. After half a block he turned and ran back to the girls.

"I'm surprised the camcorder didn't break," said Amos, and Wren jumped. She hadn't heard him come out.

"She really hates you," said Bess, her eyes wide in surprise.

"She always has," said Amos.

"She must not know that Jesus said to love one another," said Wren.

"I told her," said Amos. "But she wouldn't listen." He smiled at the kids. "Thanks for coming back. I heard her and I didn't know how to get rid of her. She's always trying to find a way inside."

"Why?" asked Wren.

"Once she gets inside, she won't leave. She'll stay put."

"You could call the police on her," said Tim.

Amos shook his head. "I wouldn't do that. Not to my sister."

Tim understood. There were times he'd wanted to call the police on his mother, but he just couldn't.

"You're bigger than she is," said Wren. "You could force her to leave."

"If I ever touched her, she'd scream to the police that I tried to beat her. She tried it before, but my friend Clyde was alive then. He saw everything, and told the policeman the truth. But now who do I have?"

"You have us," said Wren.

Amos smiled, nodded, and wiped away one tiny tear.

Buster stepped forward and licked Wren's hand. She bent down and rubbed his head. "We're friends for sure," said Wren.

3

THE NEW CLIENT

Wren lifted the camcorder from the basket on her bike and walked toward the back door of her house. Music drifted across from the Sinclair's yard along with the aroma of burritos, strong with spices.

"Hey, Bird House, I know something you don't know."

Wren spun around to find Paula Gantz standing in the shade a few feet away with a smug look on her face. Paula always used that name to make her angry. "You know a lot of things I don't." Paula was the neighborhood busybody. "What is it this time?"

Paula pressed her hands onto her waist and tilted her head. "I know who your dad's new client is."

Wren's eyes widened. "Who?" Even the family didn't always know Dad's clients.

Paula strutted forward like a peacock and stopped a foot from Wren. She waited for almost a whole minute just to tease Wren, then whispered, "Miss Brewster."

Wren almost dropped the camera. "What? Miss Brewster?

Why would our teacher need a private detective?"

Paula nodded, a knowing look on her round face. "Yes, why? She must have a big secret."

Wren didn't want to ask, but the words shot out of her mouth before she could stop them. "What is it?"

Paula frowned. "Do I know everything?"

"Usually."

"Well, I don't this time, but you can find out. You can ask your dad and then tell me."

Wren shook her head. "Dad won't tell me. It's confidential. Detectives never tell their clients' secrets. Not even to their families." Wren had asked often enough, but her dad always refused to discuss his cases or his clients with her even when she asked just to learn the business. Some day she wanted to be a famous detective like her dad, and she had to learn everything about it as soon as possible. But it wouldn't be from her dad.

The back door opened and Neil stuck his head out. "Wren, you have to come in and set the table." His voice cracked and he smiled proudly. He was thirteen, and waiting for two great things in his life: his voice to change and his growth spurt. "Mom's home already and she said to come in right now." His voice cracked twice and he beamed, then disappeared inside.

"Your mom got home early today," said Paula. "I bet she's tired of being a lawyer."

Anger churned inside Wren. "Mom likes being a lawyer."

"Well, my mom's more important. She raises money for charities."

Wren gritted her teeth to keep back an angry retort, ran to the door and stepped inside before she got even angrier and punched Paula. She knew Jesus didn't want her to hit anyone or be mean. Her chest rose and fell. She planted her back firmly against the closed door, her fists clenched and slowly counted to ten.

"In here, Wren."

Wren took a deep, steadying breath, poked her head in the kitchen and smiled at her mom. "Hi, Mom. May I take my cassette tape to Dad first?"

"Sure, but please hurry." Mrs. House was a lawyer in the law firm of Brownlee and Towns. The gray suit and silver gray blouse that she'd worn in court were covered with a heavy white butcher's apron. Her strawberry blonde hair curled prettily around her face. She had tired lines around her blue eyes. "Dinner's almost ready."

Wren ran to the inner door that led to Dad's office from the house. He also had an outside door for clients to use. The door was open and Wren knew it was all right to walk in without knocking.

Sam House sat at his large steel desk reading a report. A soup can covered with painted macaroni and filled with yellow pencils and white ball point pens sat beside his phone. Wren had made it for Father's Day last year. He looked over the top of the papers and his brown eyes crinkled in a welcoming smile. "Hi, Wren."

"Hi, Dad." She wanted to ask him about Miss Brewster, but she knew the rules. "Here's the video tape. Do you think you can help me edit it tonight?"

He shook his head regretfully. "I have something else planned for tonight, but we'll get to it the first chance I have tomorrow. Will that do?"

"Sure." She glanced quickly around for any clue about Miss Brewster. Not a clue was in sight and she bit back a sigh of regret. "Anything interesting happen today, Dad?"

Sam shrugged. "Not that I can talk about. How about you?"

"I have a lot to tell you, but Mom said I have to get right back to the kitchen." She wrinkled her small nose. "It's my turn to set the table. I should hire Philip to do it. He's always trying to find a way to make money." Philip was sixteen and had a girlfriend. He always needed money for girls, gasoline, and Clearasil.

"I don't think Philip's that desperate." Her dad picked up his report again. "Call me when it's time for me to make the salad."

Wren started out the door, then stopped abruptly and turned with wide brown eyes. Was there a mystery here? "The salad? You never make the salad. You always cook the meat."

Sam chuckled and shrugged. "We've got to be flexible. Today I'm making the salad."

Wren took a hesitant step toward Dad. "Is something going on, Dad? Something I should know about?"

"Not a thing."

Wren studied her dad closely. "Are you keeping something from me?"

"You can't make a mystery out of everything, Wren," he said with a laugh.

She flushed. She did do that a lot. "I'd better go." She turned and ran to the kitchen. "Mom, how come Dad's making the salad?"

Lorrene threw up her hands. "Don't start, Wren!"

Wren turned on the water and washed her hands. Mom didn't want her to be a detective, but some day Mom would change her mind and be proud to say that her daughter, Wren Lorrene House, was the best detective in the Midwest—or even in the whole USA.

Later she sat across the table from her brothers with Mom on one end and Dad on the other. Neil asked the blessing on the food and before Philip could say anything about his girlfriend or Neil could tell something about his computer Wren said, "We took a movie of Amos Pike today."

"That's good," said Lorrene. "Sam, did you tell Neil to take out the garbage and Philip to clean his room?"

"Did you hear your mother, boys?"

"We heard."

"Amos Pike lives on Bond Street and he has a dog named Buster."

"Pass the lasagna, Dad." Neil held his hand out, his face full of anticipation.

"Do I have to have salad, Mom?" Philip looked at the glass bowl of salad with his face wrinkled. "There are onions in it."

"Eat around the onions," his dad said helpfully.

"You have to eat salad to stay healthy," his mom added.

Wren dug out a chunk of cheese from between the noodles. "Amos Pike's sister wants to put him in an old folks' home and turn his dog in to the dog pound. Amos's teeth rattle when he talks. His dentures don't fit right."

"What are you talking about, Wren?" asked Mom.

"The movie."

"What movie?"

"You know. The one for school."

"I thought you already handed that in," said Philip. "Dad, is it all right if I use your car tonight?"

"We did film a movie, but there wasn't a tape in the camera and we didn't know it, so we had to take another one."

Sam swallowed a long drink of ice water. "You'll have to use your mother's car. I have to be gone awhile."

"Not again, Sam!" Lorrene's voice rose a little the way it usually did when she heard something she didn't want to hear. "I wanted to ask you about a case I'm working on."

"We'll talk later. I shouldn't be gone too long."

"Paula was spying again," said Wren.

"Who on this time?" asked Neil.

"Dad."

"On me?" Sam pushed back his plate. "What'd she learn?"

"Mom, may I use your car?" asked Philip as he balled his napkin.

"As long as you don't stay out later than nine thirty, Philip."

"Nine thirty! I'm not a baby, Mom. Am I, Dad?"

"It's a school night," Sam and Lorrene said together, then laughed.

"Paula said Miss Brewster was here," said Wren. She held her breath, waiting.

Sam pushed back his chair. "That's right. You tell Paula that she was definitely right about that."

"I don't think it's fair for me to do dishes alone," declared Neil. "I don't like that girl spying on us," Lorrene said, obviously preoccupied.

Wren slipped out of her chair. "Dad, about Miss Brewster . . . "

Sam lifted his hand. "Family, excuse me for a while, please. Important business." He kissed his wife and dashed out the back door, slamming it behind him.

Wren sighed, and turned to her mother. "Mom, did you talk to Miss Brewster?"

"Who?" Wren's mom asked as she picked up the empty lasagna dish.

"Miss Brewster. My teacher."

Philip raised his dark brows. "I wish she was my teacher. She's gorgeous!"

"Do I have to do dishes alone, Mom?" Neil asked, stacking the plates and making as much noise as possible.

Lorrene walked around to Neil, put her hands on his shoulders and kissed his cheek. "Neil, it's your day for the dishes. I don't want to hear another word."

Neil smiled ruefully and nodded, carrying the plates to the dishwasher.

Lorrene lifted her purse off the small table near the plant stand. "Philip, here are my car keys. Be careful and be home on time."

"Thanks, Mom." Philip kissed her and strode to the bathroom to make himself as handsome as possible. Girls always thought Wren was lucky to live in the same house as Philip, but she couldn't understand why they felt that way.

Lorrene took Wren's hand and tugged. "Let's go to the family room and talk about the movie you made today."

"What about Miss Brewster?"

"You'll have to ask your father. I didn't see her."

"So, she did see Dad! I wonder why." Wren's brain whirled and shivers of delight ran up and down her back.

"Wren," her mom said in her warning voice.

Wren shrugged, but her eyes flashed with excitement as she sank to the couch beside her mom.

4

PLANS AT SCHOOL

Wren dashed into the restroom at school with Bess right behind her. Both girls wore tan skirts with flowered blouses that they'd bought so they could dress alike. Sparks of joy shot from Wren's eyes as she stopped beside the row of sinks with her hands pressed to her racing heart. "Did you hear him, Bess?"

Bess sighed and sagged against the counter. "I heard! You're so lucky, Wren."

"Brian Davies talked to me!" Wren twirled around and stopped just before she bumped into the wastebasket. "He walked right up to me and said, 'Where's Neil?'" Wren and Bess squealed as they sank down and bobbed back up. "I don't know if I'll be able to work today!"

"I know what you mean." Bess pulled herself together. "Where is Neil?" Bess looked toward the door as if Neil would walk through any minute.

"He has a dentist appointment this morning. Dad will drop him off about ten." Wren suddenly sobered. "That reminds me. Bess, I didn't get a chance to tell you! Miss Brewster came to see my dad yesterday."

"Oh, Wren! What kind of trouble are you in?"

"I'm not!"

"I bet she didn't like the way you tried to solve the mystery of the missing globe."

Wren flushed. "Can't you forget that?"

"I wish I could!"

"I didn't know that Miss Brewster had loaned it to the seventh grade."

Bess rolled her eyes. "So, why did she want to see your dad?"

"That's just it! I don't know." Wren threw up her hands and shrugged. "Paula saw her meet with Dad and Dad admitted that she'd been there, but he wouldn't breathe a word about the meeting."

Just then the bathroom door burst open and Paula Gantz rushed in, her cheeks bright red. She wore a blue skirt with a pink and white sweater. "Wren, did you find out?"

"Find out what?" asked Bess.

Wren shook her head. "I only know that she was there and she did meet with Dad."

"What?" asked Bess.

"Miss Brewster and Dad. I just told you."

"Oh, that." Bess pulled out her brush and carefully brushed her blonde hair until it shone.

Paula frowned and jabbed her fists against her waist and glared at Wren. "I knew I should've found out on my own. I can't trust anybody!"

Wren narrowed her dark eyes and stepped up to Paula. "My dad is a professional. He does not talk about his clients."

Paula gripped Wren's arm and shrieked. "Then, she is a client! I bet she's trying to find out the truth about Mr. Abram."

"The gym teacher?" Wren frowned and tugged away from Paula. "Why should Miss Brewster want to know about Mr. Abram?"

Bess giggled. "I know."

Wren and Paula turned to stare at Bess. "You do?" they asked together in total surprise.

Bess shrugged. "Of course, I know. She's in love with Mr. Abram, but he won't ask her out. She must want your dad to find out why."

"Why doesn't she just ask Mr. Abram?" asked Paula.

"She can't do that!" cried Bess. "A woman in love shouldn't do that. I could never walk up to Neil and ask him why he won't go with me."

Paula wrinkled her nose. "The only reason you don't is because you know Neil would never talk to you again as long as you live. Neil thinks you're a little kid."

Bess's face fell. "Is that true, Wren?"

"I don't know. Maybe. Neil's more interested in his

computer than in girls."

"I asked my dad to buy me a computer," said Bess with a little pout. "He said he would in a couple of years. But I can't wait that long!"

"Forget about Neil and computers," snapped Paula. "I want to know why Miss Brewster hired Sam House."

Wren wanted to know, too, but she squared her shoulders and lifted her chin. "My dad must keep his business confidential." Wren liked the word 'confidential.' It sounded so professional, like a real detective. "And we'd better get to class before the bell rings."

"I intend to learn Miss Brewster's deep, dark secret," said Paula. She whirled around and rushed out the restroom door.

"I don't think Miss Brewster has a secret," said Bess.

"I think she does," said Wren. "And I'm going to find out what it is before Paula does."

Bess shook her finger at Wren. "You know what your mom said."

Wren hooked her hair behind her ears and tried to look very innocent. "I won't get into trouble. I just want to help Miss Brewster."

"You just want to find a mystery everywhere you look," said Bess. She sailed out of the restroom ahead of Wren and hurried down the almost deserted hall to class.

Wren looked around for Brian Davies but didn't see him. She walked slowly by the eighth-grade room, craning her neck to see inside, but she couldn't see past two boys standing in the doorway.

Later, in her own classroom, she studied Miss Brewster as she read the first chapter of John for the Bible reading for the day. Miss Brewster looked just the same as she had yesterday. Her long curly brown hair hung to her slender shoulders and down her back. She looked up, caught Wren's eye and smiled, then went back to reading. Wren desperately wanted to raise her hand and ask Miss Brewster about her problem, but she kept her hands locked in her lap just in case they acted on their own. Sometimes she did things before she knew she was going to do them.

After math class Miss Brewster said, "Today we'll plan our program for Movie Day next week. I thought it would be nice to have special music, a few recitations, and decorations as well as the movies."

Paula's hand shot up. "I'll sing."

"Thank you, Paula."

Wren waved her hand. "I'll sing, too." Wren always sang for special occasions. Before Paula had started JCA, Wren had been the best singer in the school.

"Why, thank you, Wren," said Miss Brewster with a pleased smile. "I'm thankful you girls volunteered and are willing to participate. See me later and we'll discuss the songs."

Paula glared at Wren. Wren frowned at Paula, but kept silent. Jesus wanted her to be kind and she would be kind even to Paula Gantz if it was the last thing she ever did.

Bess waved her hand in the air.

"Yes, Bess? Do you want to sing, too?" asked Miss Brewster.

Bess flushed as everyone laughed. Bess couldn't carry a tune and everyone knew it except Miss Brewster. "I want to help decorate."

"Why, thank you, Bess. This is really quite wonderful."

Bess gripped her yellow pencil tightly. "I'll be glad to help the other classes, too, say, maybe eighth grade."

"We'll see," said Miss Brewster. "Thank you."

At recess Wren caught Tim before he had a chance to join the others in a soccer game. "Tim, Miss Brewster is in big trouble."

Tim's eyes sparkled. He was always ready to do detective work. "What kind of trouble?"

"I don't know, but she hired my dad. I think we should help Dad with her case."

"I think you're right. Let's go talk to her. She just walked out the side door." Tim motioned with his head and Wren glanced toward the side of the brick building. Sure enough Miss Brewster had stepped out and was standing by herself watching the boys and girls play.

"We can't be too obvious," said Wren.

Tim nodded.

Nonchalantly Wren walked with Tim to Miss Brewster. She smiled at them and they smiled back.

"Nice day, isn't it?" asked Wren.

"Yes," said Miss Brewster.

"Did you hear about the mystery we solved for Mrs. Wheeler?" asked Tim.

Miss Brewster nodded. "I was very impressed."

"If you ever need expert help, we'd be glad to help you," said Wren.

"Why, thank you." Miss Brewster smiled from one to the other. "I'll keep that in mind."

"I don't know as much as my dad yet, but I'm learning." Wren flipped back her hair. "I watch him and listen to him and I've learned a lot already."

"I'm sure you have."

"And I read a lot," said Tim. "I can do deductive reasoning and I can follow a suspect without being spotted. Do you have a suspect you'd like me to follow?"

Miss Brewster laughed a short, tinkling laugh. "Not at the moment, but I'll keep you in mind when I do." She excused herself and walked toward two girls on the swings.

Wren looked at Tim and he nodded knowingly.

"She needs us all right," said Tim.

"I think that she's afraid to trust us with her story since we're just kids." Wren tipped her head and watched Miss Brewster laugh at something Joyce and Tina said. "We'll have to find out on our own, and then handle the problem. I think we'd better follow her home today."

Tim nodded. "I'll meet you here right after school."

The rest of the day dragged for Wren, but finally the last bell rang. She told Bess she couldn't walk home with her and ran to find Tim. Together they ducked behind the dumpster and waited for Miss Brewster. She walked out with Mr. Abram about ten minutes later.

"Here she comes," said Tim.

"With Mr. Abram." Wren held her breath and waited. "Oh, no."

"What?"

Wren saw Miss Brewster slip into her car and Mr. Abram walk to his. "We forgot about their cars." Wren's shoulders drooped as she watched the teachers drive out of the parking area and disappear out of sight down the street. "So much for following her."

"Even we can't follow a car," said Tim. He sighed heavily and walked from behind the dumpster. "I guess I'd better go home." He unlocked his ten- speed from the bike stand, said good-bye and pedaled away, the wind billowing out the back of his jacket.

Wren walked slowly away from the school, her head down. Maybe she should find out where Miss Brewster lived and watch her house to see if some mean looking character visited her.

Suddenly Paula jumped from behind a bush directly in front of Wren. Wren jumped and shrieked.

"What'd you find out?" asked Paula.

"About what?" asked Wren.

"Don't play with me," Paula declared. "I saw you talking to Miss Brewster."

"Reluctantly Wren said, "Nothing. Not a thing."

"What kind of detective are you?"

Wren's head snapped up and fire shot from her eyes. "I'm a good detective. So, there! I'm not going to give up just because I didn't learn anything today. Investigating requires a lot of leg work. I might have to do surveillance." The word slipped off her tongue as easily as it did off Dad's and she puffed up with pride.

Paula frowned as she fell into step beside Wren. "What does that mean?"

Wren shrugged. "It's a detective word, a secret word."

"You can tell me."

"Nope. I have to keep some secrets of my trade or we'd all be detectives."

Paula looked at Wren suspiciously. "I guess not," she said slowly.

"Let's get home. I have work to do." Wren flipped back her hair and raced down the sidewalk toward home.

5

TAKEOVER

On Saturday morning Wren rode to Green Street to meet Tim. Bess stayed home just in case Neil came to see her. Wren knew it would never happen and Bess knew it, too, but she continued to hope.

At Amos Pike's house Wren jumped off her bike and stared in alarm at the small brown car parked right up against the back bumper of Amos's car inside the garage. "Stella!" whispered Wren with a shiver. She ran around the house, expecting to find Stella trying to break in once again.

Tim stood at the back door with his red hair mussed and an old sweat shirt pulled down over his faded jeans. He jumped when he saw Wren, then held a finger to his lips.

"What's going on?" whispered Wren.

"Stella's inside. She took over the house."

"How?"

Anger flashed in his eyes. "She was already inside

when I got here. I saw her through the window. She better not have hurt Amos or Buster!" Tim shivered and took a step back from the door. "I don't know how she got inside. I've been waiting for you before I knocked."

"Where's Amos?"

"Inside, I guess."

"Where's Buster?"

"I don't know. Do you think she's already sent him to the dog pound?"

Wren wrinkled her brow and tapped her finger against her chin. "It's time to do some deductive reasoning. This is Saturday and the dog pound is closed today."

Tim relaxed a little. "And we talked to Amos on the phone last night and he was looking forward to seeing us today."

"So, she wouldn't have had time to put Buster in the pound. He must be hiding around here somewhere. We know he can't be inside since Stella's there." Wren walked around a clump of bushes. "Buster! Here, Buster!" She waited, but didn't hear even a faint bark. A bird chirped and fluttered from one branch to another.

"I hope she didn't hurt him," said Tim.

"I'm going to knock on the door and ask to see Amos." Wren marched forward, a determined look on her face.

Tim caught her arm. "Wait!"

She frowned and shook his hand off. "What?"

"We've got to have a plan."

Wren nodded and grinned, barely able to stand still. "You're right, of course." Cool wind blew against her and she hunched into her jacket. "A plan! We've got to think of something." She thought and thought while Tim stood beside her, thinking too. Finally she turned to Tim, her eyes sparkling. "I have it!"

"What? What?"

As quickly as she could Wren outlined the plan with Tim adding ideas now and then.

A few minutes later Wren hid at the corner of the house while Tim ran to the front door. He lifted his fist and knocked five loud raps. Wren's heart raced and she shivered. From a branch of the tree beside her a squirrel cracked a nut and dropped part of the shell to the grass. Wren jumped as if a firecracker had gone off under her feet.

Stella opened the door and frowned down at Tim. "I don't want a newspaper."

"I'm not selling papers."

Suddenly Stella screamed and shook her thick pink finger at Tim. The nail was covered with bright red polish. "I know you. You were here with the movie camera the other day. Get away from here and leave me alone. Shoo!" She tried to chase him away as if he were a dog.

He stood bravely before her, his face set. "I came to see Amos."

"He doesn't want to see you." Her face turned as red

as her nails. "He's taking a nap and he doesn't want to be disturbed."

"Amos takes his nap just after lunch and it's only eleven."

Stella pushed against the door.

"Wait!" Tim caught the screen door and held it open. She glared at him. "What's wrong now?"

"I wanted to show Amos something I found in the grass. It glitters like a diamond."

"Really?" She hesitated. "Show it to me."

"I left it in the grass." He motioned toward the street.

"Well, go get it and bring it here."

Tim shook his head. "I don't want to touch it in case I leave my fingerprints on it and get blamed for stealing it."

Stella pushed the door wider and stepped outside. She tugged her sweater close around her thick waist. "Show me where it is right now."

Tim hid a grin as he led Stella down the sidewalk past the straggly row of marigolds toward the lawn next to the curb.

Wren saw her chance and dashed around the corner of the house and silently, stealthily slipped inside. The screen door squeaked a little and she held her breath, but Stella was too busy following Tim around.

The house was warm and smelled of brewing coffee. A purse lay on the table with a folded newspaper beside it.

"Amos!" Wren called softly. "Buster! It's me, Wren."

She dashed to the closed doors and opened them one at a time. The bedroom was empty. She looked inside the bathroom and even the closet. Amos was not there. Buster wasn't either. She poked her head inside the basement door and called, "Amos! Are you down there? It's me, Wren." There was no answer; only the smell of dust. She stopped in the middle of the kitchen, her hand at her throat. Where was Amos Pike? What had happened to him? Had Stella put him in an old folks home like Amos said she would?

At the front door Stella said, "Get away from this house, little boy! That's just a piece of broken glass!"

"But it sparkled just like a diamond."

"Well, it isn't! Now get away from here!" Stella slammed the door just as Wren slipped out the back door, her heart in her mouth.

Wren dashed around the corner of the house and sank weakly to the grass. Tim dropped down beside her, his face as red as his hair.

"Well?" he asked.

"He wasn't inside and neither was Buster!"

"Maybe she killed them both and buried their bodies!"

"Don't even think that!" Twice that she knew about her dad had found dead bodies. That part of detective work frightened her.

"Then where is Amos Pike?"

"I don't know, but I think we'd better find him."

"What nursing home did he say she was going to put him in?"

She wrinkled her forehead in thought and replayed that conversation in her mind. "Retirement Village!"

"Yes. Yes, I remember." Tim jumped up and motioned to Wren. "Let's go to my place and call them to see if Amos is there."

Wren nodded, then ran to her bike and followed Tim to his tiny house on Bond Street. She'd never been inside his house and she wondered if he'd let her in now.

Tim faced her, flushing to the roots of his red hair so that his freckles blended into each other. "My mom is home."

"So?"

"So, you can't come in."

"Why?"

"She yells and swears at me and I don't want you to hear. You wouldn't want to hear all the bad words she says."

Wren glanced toward the run-down house and nodded. She didn't want to hear Tim's mom yell or swear, and she didn't want Tim to be embarrassed because she was there. "I'll wait here while you call."

"I'll be out in a minute." Tim propped his bike against the house and ran inside, closing the door with a gentle click.

Wren sank to the front step and sat with her chin in her hands. A weak sun shone overhead. An ant crawled over the toe of her tennis shoe. Down the street children screamed over who owned a football.

Finally the door opened and Tim stepped out, once again closing the door quietly. "He's not at Retirement Village and he's not at Johnson Nursing Home. I didn't try any of the other places."

"I think we should go back and talk to Stella. This time I'll talk to her."

"It's worth a try."

Wren pedaled after Tim and at Amos's place they parked their bikes on the far side of the garage out of Stella's sight. Tim hid at the side of the house while Wren ran to the door.

Taking a deep breath to steady her shaking hand, Wren knocked and waited. When the door opened, Stella stood there with a frown on her found face. Wren said, "Hello, I came to see my friend Amos Pike. Would you tell him I'm here, please."

"He's not here. He went to buy groceries."

"But his car is still in the garage."

Stella's eyes darkened. "He rode with a friend. I'll tell him you were here."

"Never mind. I'll just sit here and wait." Wren crossed her arms and plopped down on the step, her face set.

Stella stepped out with an angry, mean expression on her face. "Get away from here! Amos doesn't want kids hanging around his place!"

"But I'm his friend."

"He said he didn't want kids here trampling his flowers!"

"He didn't mean me." Wren didn't budge.

Stella bent down and hissed, "Get away from here right now! I mean it!"

Slowly Wren stood. "Tell me where to find Amos and I'll go meet him. Is he shopping at The Grocer or did he go to SaveMor?"

Stella threw up her hands. "How should I know? Now, get out of here!"

"Well, I don't know." Wren put on her dumbest face. Sometimes she could act as if she didn't know anything at all. "I think I should stay here. Don't you think I should stay here?"

Stella sputtered angrily, and Wren knew Tim was enjoying the entire scene. Stella slammed the screen door and stood looking through the tiny wires. "I want you off my property now or I'll call the police."

Wren tucked her hair behind her ears. "I didn't know this place was yours. I thought it belonged to Amos."

"Well, it doesn't. Now get away from here."

Wren sighed and walked slowly down the sidewalk. When the door slammed she turned, then dashed to Tim's side. "What do you think?"

"I don't know. Amos isn't inside. I think we should ask the neighbors if they saw anything."

Wren agreed and they ran to the neighbors' house on the left. No one was home so they ran to the neighbors' house on the right. An old woman opened the door a crack.

"I don't want none," she said in a voice that cracked worse than Neil's.

"We're not selling anything," said Wren. "My name is Wren and this is Tim. We're looking for our friend Amos Pike, but he's not at home."

"He asked us to visit him this morning," said Tim.

"He's not home for sure," said the woman. She opened the door wider. A cat curled around her legs and settled for a nap on her slippered foot. "That woman that's always skulking around his house is there and Amos took off at a run with his dog."

Wren shot a look at Tim, then turned back to the woman. "He took off?"

The woman nodded. "She wouldn't even let him take his car, she wouldn't."

"Where would he go?" asked Tim.

"I don't know," said the woman. "He has no friends."

Wren tapped her chest. "Yes, he does! He has us."

"I'm glad to hear that. He needs help, that's for sure."

Wren smiled. "Thanks for your help. We'll tell Amos that you helped us when we find him."

"You do that. And you tell him I did return that book that he says I still have."

"We'll tell him," said Tim.

Wren didn't say anything until the door closed. "Tim, I think he'll try to find us. Let's get back to your house and see."

Several minutes later Tim walked out of his house once again, his shoulders drooping. "He came here and Mom sent him away. He came even before we were here to use the phone, but Mom didn't tell me. I called your house and he's not there. I wonder where he is."

Wren sighed loud and long. She looked up at the gray sky. "Please, heavenly Father, take care of our friend Amos Pike wherever he is."

6

THE SEARCH

With her head down Wren walked to her bike. She turned to Tim with a thoughtful frown. "You know, Tim, I think God sent us to Amos Pike."

Tim nodded, his face very sober. "I think we can help Amos and God knew it even last week when we were here."

"Somehow, we must help him!" Her voice rose and she gulped, then took a deep breath. "Right now we know that Amos is not in his house. We know that he came here this morning to see you. Probably to get your help."

"Probably. I wish I would've been here!" He shoved his hands deep into the pockets of his jeans. "At least we know he's not in a nursing home locked away."

"That's one good thing." Wren looked to her right and left, ahead and behind her. "He's out here somewhere. But where?"

"Yeah—where?"

Wren straddled her bike. "First let's ride toward my house. You can take one route and I'll take another in case we run across him heading for Lyons Street. We'll meet later at my place— hopefully with Amos."

"Or make a new plan if we have to," said Tim in a low, sad voice.

"If we have to," agreed Wren. "Let's get going."

Tim nodded, told her the route he'd take and pedaled away with his thin back hunched over the handlebars, his head up and his bright red hair blowing in the breeze.

Wren hooked her dark hair behind her ears. Dark bangs almost touched her brows. She pedaled back to Green Street and over to Maple, alert for any sign of Amos or Buster. At a tall white house she heard a dog barking wildly in the back yard. She stopped, her heart hammering. "Buster?" she whispered as she pedaled up the drive and around back. But the dog was huge, brown and white with long hair. "It's not Buster," she said with a heavy sigh. Wren pedaled back to the street and continued on her way without spotting Amos or Buster. Close to her house she saw Jane Osborn and Susan Sinclair sitting on the porch of Jane's house and rode up to them.

"Hi, Wren," they said together. "Want to play with us?"

"Not today, thanks." Wren straddled her bike.

"I'm looking for Amos Pike. He's real old and has gray hair and blue eyes and a small black dog named Buster."

"We didn't see him," said Jane.

"Are you playing detective again, Wren?" asked Susan with a giggle.

Wren flushed. "I'm not playing! I am a detective and someday I'll be as good as my dad!"

"Little girls can't be detectives," said Jane.

"Or they'd have a series on TV about it," added Susan.

Wren rode away without a backward glance.

What did they know about being a detective? She could be one if she wanted, and she didn't have to wait until she was old.

At her house she found Tim waiting in the back yard on the picnic table. The shade of the tall maple kept the sun off him. He jumped to the ground when he saw her. "Well?"

"Nothing."

His shoulder slumped and he hoisted himself back up on the table. "That's too bad."

She peeled off her jacket and dropped it beside him. "You?"

"Nothing. He's not here either. I already asked. Nobody saw him. Nobody saw anybody." Tim sounded and look discouraged.

"We have to find him!" Wren exclaimed. "I'll see if Bess will go with us to look."

"Want to go now?"

Wren's stomach growled and she laughed. "Let's eat lunch first. Want to?"

Tim hesitated, then shrugged. "I guess so."

"Chicken sandwiches and a salad."

His eyes lit up and he nodded. Wren knew he would've had a bowl of corn flakes and a piece of toast. "Will your mom mind if I eat with you?"

"Why should she?" He shrugged. "I never eat anywhere but home."

Wren smiled. "Mom will like having you, Tim. She'll ask you a lot of questions. She always does. That's because she's a lawyer."

Tim squirmed uneasily. "What kind of questions?"

"Oh, she'll probably ask what you want to be when you grow up."

"A detective."

Wren made a face. "Better not tell her that."

"What else will she ask?"

"If you plan to attend college after high school. She's big on that."

"Do you have to go to college to be a detective?"

You have to study almost what the police study and you have to work with a detective or the police for awhile to get training.

Tim frowned. "So, what's the answer about going to college?"

Wren thought for a long time. "Well, if you want to go to college, tell her and that'll make her happy."

"All right."

She led him inside and showed him the bathroom where he could wash. "When you're finished come to the kitchen. I'll be there." She saw the uncertain look on his face and she smiled. "It really is all right if you're here. Mom and Dad like you. You might even get Dad to tell why Miss Brewster was here."

His eyes brightened and he nodded. "Yeah, maybe!" He slipped into the bathroom and she ran to the kitchen to find her dad making lunch.

"Hi," she said as she watched him smear salad dressing on whole wheat bread.

"Hi." He smiled, then bent down and kissed her cheek. "What great secrets are hidden behind those huge brown eyes?"

She laughed. "Not as many as are hidden behind your brown eyes." She picked up a piece of white meat and popped it into her mouth, savoring the tender, moist bite. "Tim Avery's staying for lunch."

"Oh?"

"Is that all right?"

Sure. Just as long as you two keep your detective talk out of the conversation so your mother doesn't get upset."

"We'll try." She glanced over her shoulder as Tim hesitantly walked in. "Tim, want a piece of chicken?"

His eyes lit up.

"Sure." Sam smiled back at Tim. "Hi. We're glad to have you with us today. Wren always likes company on the days she has to set the table."

"Dad!"

Sam winked at her and she giggled.

"He was only teasing, Tim," she said.

"I know." Tim watched as Wren opened the silverware drawer and pulled out forks for the salad. "But I'll help set the table."

"For five," said Sam. "Philip isn't here."

"Where is he?" asked Wren.

"He went to see about a job as carryout boy at SaveMor. Sally started working there yesterday and he wants to be close to her, he says." Sam chuckled. "Little does he know that he'll be working too hard to have time for her."

"Maybe it's enough just to see her," said Wren, thinking about Brian Davies.

"Maybe." Sam washed and dried his hands, then squeezed Tim's shoulder. "Aren't you glad you're too young for girl problems?"

Tim nodded. "I just like detective problems." He glanced at Wren, then looked back up at Sam. "We told Miss Brewster we'd help her if she ever needed help. I told her I could follow a suspect without being spotted."

"That's quite a feat." Sam cut a cucumber into a bowl with full concentration.

"We'd help her all we could," said Wren, watching her dad closely.

"That's good," said Sam, slicing a tomato on top of the cucumber.

Wren looked at Tim and he looked at her and they

both shrugged. Wren set plates on the table and Tim set the silverware beside them.

"I hear you're looking for Amos Pike," said Sam.

Wren nodded. "I hope nothing bad happened to him."

Just then Lorrene walked in with Neil behind her. "I see lunch is almost ready. Great." She kissed Wren and patted Tim on the head. "Hi, kids. I'm hungry."

"Hi, Tim," said Neil. "I see Wren got you to do all of her work."

"I did not!" cried Wren.

"She didn't," said Tim.

"Neil, don't tease your sister," said Lorrene as she lifted two bottle of salad dressing from the refrigerator door. Neil carried the salad to the table while Wren filled glasses with ice water. Tim helped her set them in place while Sam and Lorrene chatted about their plans for the afternoon.

Several minutes later as they all ate, Lorrene looked at Tim and smiled. "What do you want to be when you grow up, Tim?"

Tim shot a look at Wren and she bit back a giggle. "I'd like to go to college," he said almost in one word.

"That's good." Lorrene looked pleased. "Isn't that good, Wren?"

Wren nodded as she bit off a huge piece of her sandwich so she wouldn't have to say anything for a while.

Neil held his fork in mid-air, a piece of lettuce speared on the tips. "Dad, I finished the computer check you wanted."

"Great, Neil."

"I wish your computer could help us find Amos Pike," said Tim.

"Why is it so important to find him?" asked Lorrene.

Wren almost choked, but Tim answered easily, "He's our friend and we had a meeting with him this morning. He wasn't at home."

"He's the man in our movie for school," said Wren. "Remember, Mom? I told you about his marigolds, and you said it would be nice if I took him a bouquet of flowers."

"I remember. I'm sure he'll turn up." Lorrene sipped her water, then dabbed her mouth with the white paper napkin that Wren had put on the table.

"I have a question for you, Mom," said Wren.

"Yes?" Lorrene looked pleased.

"A lawyer question."

Sam laughed. "This is quite a switch, Wren."

Wren flushed. "I need to know how someone, say a woman named Stella, could just move right into her brother's house and kick him out? Would Stella be able to stay in her brother's house just like it was her own?"

"Of course not!"

Wren nodded. "What if she locked the brother out?"

Lorrene looked closely at Wren. "Are you involved in something again, Wren? Am I going to get upset?"

"It's a problem we have to figure out," spoke up Tim, and Wren breathed easier.

"A hypothetical problem for school!" Lorrene smiled and relaxed. "Good. It's good to use your mind that way."

Wren didn't want to lie so she didn't say anything. A few minutes later she excused herself and Tim followed.

Outdoors she turned to Tim. "Let's get Bess and some of the others to help us find Amos."

Tim nodded. "Maybe with all of us working together, we'll find him before night."

"It would be terrible if he was locked out of his house overnight! Where would he go?" Wren shuddered. "Once I saw an old man sleeping on a park bench with an old ragged rug over him."

"We gotta find him, Wren!"

"I know. Let's go get Bess."

"Then check the park," whispered Tim.

"The park," said Wren.

7

THE PARK

Shivers ran down her spine as Wren walked her bike to the sidewalk with Bess and Tim behind her. They just had to find Amos Pike in the park!

Just then Paula Gantz jumped from her porch and ran across the street, her jacket flapping. She blocked Wren's way. "Where are you going?" she asked in an accusing voice.

"To find Amos Pike," said Tim.

"Do you know where he is?" asked Wren. "You always know everything."

Paula frowned. "I don't even know Amos Pike. Who is he? Why don't I know him?"

"He lives on Green Street," said Bess.

Paula made a face. "No wonder I don't know him. That's the slum part of town."

"It is not!" cried Tim.

"You're saying that because you live near there," said Paula. "But it is slum. It stinks and looks ugly. I always roll the car window up and lock the door if we have to drive through there."

"Let's go," said Wren. She'd had enough of Paula.

"Why do you want to find this Amos Pike?" asked Paula, catching Wren's handlebar so she couldn't ride away.

"He's missing," said Paula, her dark eyes flashing with excitement. "I want to see Amos Pike and find out what the mystery is all about."

Wren frowned. Paula could make trouble with her nosy interfering. "Who says there's a mystery?"

"There has to be for you to be this excited." Paula laughed and tugged her sweater down over her jeans.

"That's the truth," said Bess under her breath.

"Wait for me," said Paula. "I'll get my bike and be right back." She dashed across the street, stopped and spun around to face Wren. "You'd better wait for me! I mean it!"

Wren sighed heavily. "We'll wait. We can use all the help we can get."

"Even Paula's," whispered Tim, and Bess giggled.

Several minutes later Wren rode into the park with the others behind her. A bright sun warmed the sidewalks. Pigeons flew from the top of a storage shed down to the ground. Boys and girls played on the swings and slides and soccer field. An old man sat on a green bench and Wren's heart leaped. She pedaled toward him shouting, "Amos!"

He turned to face her. Long gray whiskers covered his chin and hung to his thin chest. "Who're you calling Amos?" the man asked in a mean voice.

"I . . . I thought you were Amos Pike." She flushed to the roots of her brown hair.

"Do I look like Amos Pike?"

"Do you know him?" asked Tim.

"Sure. I don't like him, but I know him."

"Why don't you like him?" asked Paula, pushing around the others, her nose almost twitching in the excitement of hearing the answer.

"It doesn't matter," cut in Wren just as the man started to speak. "Do you know where he is?"

"At home probably," said the man.

"He's not," said Bess. "His sister took over his house."

Tim and Wren frowned at Bess and she shrugged innocently.

The man tugged on his whiskers. "That old man don't have no sister."

Wren's stomach tightened. Who was Stella if she wasn't his sister? "Are you sure?"

The man nodded. "Don't I look like I know what I'm talking about?"

"Do you know where he would be if he wasn't at home?" asked Tim.

"Do I look like I know everything?" The man awkwardly pushed himself up. "Now, get away from me and leave me to enjoy my walk in the park."

Wren watched him limp away, then she turned to the others. "We must find Amos Pike. Let's fan out and look everywhere. Behind every bush and tree, everywhere!"

"We'll find him," said Tim.

"We have to," answered Wren.

"I bet I find him first," said Paula. "I always see everything."

Wren couldn't argue with that.

Bess tugged Wren's arm. "Look," she whispered, her eyes sparkling. "It's Neil. And Brian."

Wren's heart fluttered.

Tim frowned at the girls. "Are you going to look for Amos, or not?"

"I'll look over there," said Bess, pointing to the area where Neil stood with Brian. With a little giggle she pedaled off.

"I'm going to look around the bandstand," said Paula. She dodged around a group of girls.

Tim touched Wren's arm. "Do you think Amos lied to us about Stella?"

Wren bit her bottom lip. "I don't know. We'll have to find out."

"His neighbor said Stella was his sister."

Wren brightened. "That's right! I'd rather believe Amos than that stranger."

Tim cleared his throat. "Amos is almost a stranger."

Wren nodded with a sigh. "What is the truth?"

"We'll have to find that out."

"We're detectives and we can do it!"

"We won't find Amos just standing here," said Tim.

Wren nodded. "I'll take that end of the park and you take the other."

Wren searched her area without finding Amos, then rode to join Bess who was watching Neil and Brian play tennis.

"Neil will win," whispered Bess proudly.

"I think Brian will," whispered back Wren. "Neil missed that last ball."

Bess nudged Wren. "Look who's coming."

Wren glanced back to see Wendy, an eighth grade girl who liked Brian.

"Hey, Bird House!" called Wendy.

Wren shot a look at Brian to see if he laughed, but he didn't and she was able to turn to face Wendy. "Hi, Wendy."

Wendy stopped a foot away and glared at Wren. "Don't you think Brian is tired of you watching him?"

"Am I watching him?"

"You know you are. Everybody knows you love him!"

Wren burned with embarrassment. She didn't dare look to see if Brian had heard Wendy. "I happened to be looking for Amos Pike."

"Then why don't you go do it and leave Brian alone?"

Wren ducked her head and walked her bike around a bush out of sight of Brian. "Oh, Bess! What'll I do now?"

"Maybe he didn't hear Wendy."

"He heard! I just know it. I can't face Brian again as long as I live!"

Bess nodded sympathetically. "But maybe Brian will forget Wendy said anything."

"Maybe." But Wren doubted it.

Just then Paula ran to them. She'd left her bike near a tree. Her face was bright with excitement. She slid to a stop just inches from Wren. "I saw her!"

"Who?"

"Miss Brewster! I saw her!" Paula took a deep breath. "She's sitting on a bench over there with Mr. Abram. I tried to listen in on them, but she spotted me and I ran. She was crying!"

"Oh my!" exclaimed Bess.

Wren dropped her bike to the grass. "I'll take care of this."

Bess caught her arm. "Don't get into trouble."

"Me?"

"And if you do, don't you get me in trouble with you."

"Me neither," said Paula.

Wren pulled away from Bess and dashed across the grass toward the secluded spot that Paula had spoken about. A squirrel zipped up a tree to get away from her. She stopped behind a bush and peeked around it. The teachers sat on the bench, hand in hand, talking too low for her to hear.

"What're you doing?" whispered Tim, and she jumped.

"I'm trying to find out what Miss Brewster is talking about. I know we should be looking for Amos, but I didn't think it would hurt to take time out for Miss Brewster."

"We'll have to get closer to hear." Tim pushed his red hair off his forehead. It slipped right back down.

"It's risky, Tim. There's no cover between here and there."

He grinned. "We can do it."

She frowned. "Not we. Me. I'm going alone. It's easier for one to sneak up and eavesdrop than two." She knew he wanted to go with her, but finally he nodded.

Stealthily she crept toward the back of the bench, careful not to step on the twigs in the soft grass. One snap of a twig would give her away. Her nose tickled and she pinched it. One sneeze would give her away, too. She trembled at the thought.

Miss Brewster and Mr. Abram sat with their heads together, her brown curly hair against his short black hair.

"It must work out, Josh," she was saying as Wren stopped a foot away from them.

"But things don't always work out," he said.

She sighed heavily. "I know." She was quiet a long time. "We prayed, and I know God will answer."

"Then it's wrong to worry about it." He turned her

face to his and kissed her. Wren stood motionless, suddenly afraid they'd spot her.

Miss Brewster glanced back and Wren wanted to shrink down to an inch high so she could hide behind the leaves at her feet.

Miss Brewster jumped up with Mr. Abram beside her. "Wren, what are you doing?"

Wren flushed painfully.

Paula dashed around the bushes. "She was spying on you."

"Wren!" Miss Brewster shook her finger at Wren. "How dare you do such a thing!"

"Your parents will hear about this, young lady!" Mr. Abram scowled and Wren trembled.

"She only wanted to help," said Tim, stepping close to Wren as if to protect her.

"That's right," said Bess.

"Help with what?" asked Mr. Abram.

"With the problem," said Paula. "Wren is a detective and she wants to solve the problem that Miss Brewster went to see Wren's dad about."

Miss Brewster frowned.

"What problem, Meg?" asked Mr. Abram, looking into her eyes.

She shook her head and sighed. "Wren House, you and your detective work."

Wren wasn't sure whether she should be proud or

embarrassed. Miss Brewster leaned down toward Wren. "I went to see your dad to pick up some pictures that he developed for me."

Wren glared at Paula and Paula looked very innocent.

"Why didn't you tell us?" asked Wren.

"It wasn't your business," said Miss Brewster.

Paula tossed her head. "I knew Wren would get in trouble again. She's so nosy!"

"Look who's talking," said Tim.

"I'm going to speak to your parents about your eavesdropping, Wren," said Miss Brewster. "I know that they'll want to deal with it before it goes any further. You must learn to respect other people's privacy."

Wren twisted her toe in the grass. Her stomach knotted. She watched Miss Brewster and Mr. Abram walk away.

"I should've known there was no mystery," said Paula.

"But you're the one who said there was!" Wren glared at Paula.

"I suppose this story about Amos Pike is all made up, too," said Paula. "I won't help anymore!" Before anyone could speak she ran to her bike and pedaled away.

Bess took a deep breath. "Wren, you did it again."

"It wasn't your fault," said Tim. "You really thought there was a mystery to solve. You were only trying to help."

"That's right! I was." Wren shivered. "I hope Miss Brewster forgets about telling Mom and Dad."

"She won't," said Bess.

Just then a small, black dog ran around the bushes and barked wildly.

"Buster!" cried Wren. "Tim, it's Buster!"

"He'll lead us to Amos!" said Tim.

Bess grabbed Wren's arm. "Don't you dare follow that dog! There is no mystery with Amos Pike just like there was no mystery with Miss Brewster."

Wren hesitated, suddenly uncertain. Was Bess right?

"Come on, Wren," said Tim, running toward Buster.

"If you go, Wren, I won't go with you," said Bess.

Wren looked at Bess and then at Tim and Buster. "I have to go, Bess! I have to find Amos Pike."

8

BUSTER

"Where did Buster go?" Wren frantically called to Tim.

Tim slowed and glanced back at Wren. "I saw him run around that yellow house."

They rode around the house through tall grass.

"Amos! Can you hear me? Buster! Here, Buster!" Wren called.

"Amos! It's Tim. And Wren. Where are you?"

Wren stopped and straddled her bike as she looked up and down the sidewalk. "Buster! Here, Buster. Come here, boy."

Suddenly the back door of the yellow house opened and an old woman stuck her head out the door. "You kids get away from here. Don't cut across my yard again or I'll call the police on you."

Wren trembled. She hated to be yelled at. "We're sorry. We saw a little black dog run through here and we're trying to find him."

"Don't let your dog run across my yard either!"

The woman peered closely at Wren and Tim. "Is it your dog?"

Tim hesitated. "No. He belongs to Amos Pike. We have to find Amos. Do you know him?"

The woman stepped out of her door, but kept one hand on the storm door to keep it open. She was small, frail, and wrinkled. "I knew his dear wife very well, but I lost track of him after she passed on. Is something wrong with Amos?"

Wren nodded. "We think so." She didn't know how much to tell the old woman. "I'm Wren and this is Tim. We're friends of Amos. We want to find him and talk to him."

"I'm Mina Thomkins." She let the door close and stood with her arms folded over her thin breast. "I hope you find Amos. But if he doesn't want to be found, you won't find him. He likes a good joke." The woman chuckled and nodded her silver head. "He always was one for practical jokes."

Wren groaned. Could Amos be playing a joke on them?

"Does he have a sister named Stella?" asked Tim.

Mina Thomkins shrugged slightly. "That I can't say. I knew his wife, but I didn't know much about Amos. Except his joking, of course."

"Did you see his dog Buster go through your yard?" asked Wren.

"I saw the little dog, but I didn't see where it went." Mina Thomkins shivered. "I'd better get back inside before I catch a chill. You children remember to stay out of my yard. I don't want a path worn through my grass."

"We didn't mean to hurt it," said Wren. "We just needed to follow Buster." She looked around at the long grass. "If you need help mowing your lawn, we can do it for you sometime."

The woman's eyes brightened, then she shook her head. "Thanks anyway. My grandson comes once a week and mows for me. He couldn't make it last week, but I'm sure he'll be here today. He wouldn't want me to have someone else do it."

"If he doesn't come by Monday after school, we'll do it," said Tim.

"If you don't mow it soon, it'll be too hard to mow and you'll have to rake it," said Wren. Twice she'd forgotten to mow on time and had had to rake the entire lawn.

Mina Thomkins cleared her throat and blushed. "I don't have money to pay for lawn mowing."

"We wouldn't charge you," said Wren. "We like helping people."

Mrs. Thomkins smiled. "That's wonderful. I raised my three youngsters to be helpful, but sometimes lately I think people in this world walk through life doing only for themselves without a care for others." Mina Thomkins dabbed a tear from her pale blue eyes. "You are good children. If you aren't too busy sometime, come visit me. I'll make you popcorn. Do you like popcorn?"

"I do," said Tim. Sometimes he ate a bowl of popcorn for supper.

"I do, too," said Wren. Neil made the popcorn at home. He always knew just how much butter to dribble on it to make it perfect.

"Good-bye, children. I hope you find Amos Pike." Mina Thomkins slipped inside and closed her door with a quiet snap.

Wren sighed as she walked her bike back to the sidewalk. "Now what are we going to do, Tim? We lost Buster."

"Let's look a little longer before we give up." Tim pedaled along the sidewalk in the direction of Amos's house.

"Tim?"

He glanced back at Wren. Her front bike tire was almost touching his back tire. "What?"

She didn't know if she could say the words, but she did anyway. "What if Amos is playing a joke on us? What if everything is a joke? His sister, everything?"

"I don't know." Tim's shoulders slumped. "I've been thinking the same thing. Maybe we should ride to his house and see if he's home."

"Let's do." Wren followed Tim down the sidewalk and stopped beside him just outside Amos's house. She pointed to the car outside the garage. "Stella's car is still there."

"I see it." He leaned his bike against the side of the

garage away from the house. "You knock on the front door and I'll run around and knock on the back door. If Amos and Stella are both inside, one will answer the front door and the other the back."

"Amos had better not be tricking us." Wren rode her bike up to the house, rested it against the edge of the step and jumped up to stand at the door. She waited, her heart in her mouth, until she was sure Tim was at the back door, then she knocked.

Stella pulled open the door and Wren jumped. Stella scowled in anger and Wren wanted to run away, but she didn't. "What're you doing back here, little girl?"

"Is Amos home yet?" The words squeaked out and Wren flushed.

"No! He's probably still shopping. Now, get out of here!"

"Are you his sister?"

"Yes. What business is it of yours?"

Just then Wren heard Tim knock on the back door. "Someone's at your back door."

"I can hear."

"I want to talk to you more, can I step inside and wait until you answer the door?" Wren took a step forward and reached for the door knob.

Stella looked toward the back door angrily, then turned back to Wren. "Don't touch that door! Get away from here!"

Wren put on her innocent look. "Maybe it's Amos. Maybe he's playing a joke on you."

"He's always playing jokes, but he won't play another one on me!" Stella slammed the door and a few seconds later Wren heard her yell at Tim and slam the back door. Wren grabbed her bike and walked it out of sight behind the garage where she waited for Tim to join her.

"He's not inside," said Tim with a long, loud sigh.

"I really didn't think he would be." Wren absently rubbed the white tape on her handlebars. "Let's ride around the neighborhood and see if we spot Buster again."

Tim hiked up his faded jeans. "You take that block and I'll take this one. We'll meet back here in a little while."

With a small nod Wren rode away, looking and listening for Buster. She dodged a girl on a bike and frowned at a puppy that yapped at her tire.

Suddenly without warning, Buster poked his head around a bush. She jerked to a stop and almost fell off her bike. "Buster!" she called. "Come here!"

He barked and ran to her.

"Buster, we've been looking all over for you. Where's Amos?" She reached out to him, but before she could touch him he turned and ran again. She rode after him, her heart beating wildly against her ribcage. Her mouth felt cotton dry.

Buster crossed the street and Wren started after him. A blue car honked and she slid to a stop, impatiently waiting for the car to pass. She gripped her handlebar until her knuckles turned white. Finally she rode across the street just in time to see Buster cut across someone's back yard. After being yelled at by Mina Thomkins Wren was afraid to ride across lawns. She leaned forward and whizzed down the sidewalk, almost colliding with a small boy on a tricycle. "Sorry," she said and kept going.

Buster cut across another yard, this time heading back toward Green Street.

"Where are you going?" cried Wren in frustration.

Buster didn't look back and soon was out of sight running through back yards. Once a man yelled at him, but he kept going, his small, black ears held high.

Wren sped around the block and stopped at the spot where she thought Buster would come through. He was nowhere in sight. "Oh, Buster, Buster," she whispered. She cupped her hands around her mouth and shouted, "Buster! Amos! Where are you?"

She listened, her head tilted, but all she heard was a car on the street and music drifting out from a two story frame house that needed painting. She pushed back her bangs and hooked her hair over her ears. With a tired sigh she pedaled to meet Tim.

"Did you find him?" she asked. He looked tired and discouraged.

"No. You?"

"I saw Buster, but lost him." She pointed and told Tim

exactly where she'd seen Buster. "I can't look any more today. I have to get home."

"Me, too. See you tomorrow in church."

"Tomorrow." She blinked back tears. "I hate to give up! What about Amos Pike? Where is he going to sleep tonight?"

"He'll be all right. We'll pray for him."

She nodded, silently praying as she rode toward home. Maybe she could get her dad to drive her around after dinner to look for Amos.

Later at the dinner table, she asked, "Dad could you drive me around the streets so I can look for Amos Pike?"

Before he could answer, Mom shook her head and frowned. "Wren, you've done enough detective work for one day."

Wren squirmed. "What do you mean, Mom?"

"Miss Brewster called."

Wren kept her head down. She wanted to sink out of sight under the table. "Oh."

Lorrene House sighed loud and long. "Wren, when will you learn? You must not spy on others! I've told you that over and over and over."

"I thought she needed help," said Wren.

"You were wrong," said dad. "You hurt your teachers with your spying and you embarrassed us."

Tears stung Wren's eyes. Dad's scoldings always made her feel terrible.

Lorrene set down her glass of water. "Wren, go to your room and stay there. No TV tonight."

Wren's head shot up. "But . . . "

"I agree, Wren," said dad.

"What about . . . about Amos Pike?" she asked in a small voice.

"What about him?" asked dad.

Wren looked helplessly at her dad. "Amos is missing, Dad. I don't know where he'll spend the night since he can't get inside his house."

Her mom pressed her fingertips to her temples. "Don't do this to me, Wren."

"Please, Mom, just listen to me! Amos is in trouble. I just know it!"

Lorrene House walked around to Wren and took her hand. "Honey, you have a great imagination. You must learn to use it wisely."

"He's in trouble, Mom."

"Just like Miss Brewster?"

Wren flushed.

"Wren was right about the Wheeler Place," said dad.

Wren's mom nodded and squeezed her hand. "I know. But, Sam, that was one time out of how many?"

"I'm right this time, Mom! Honest." She turned to her dad, her dark eyes wide and pleading. "I am right, Dad! I know I am. I'd stake my reputation as a detective on it."

Lorrene threw up her hands and her brothers laughed.

Sam House leaned toward Wren. "You are not a detective, Wren," he said gently.

Her shoulders drooped and tears filled her eyes. How could Dad say she wasn't a real detective?

She walked to Dad and put her hand on his strong shoulder. "You might think I'm not a detective, but I am right about Amos Pike!" Her voice dropped. "I think."

"I won't take you out to look for him, Wren. Help with the dishes and then go right to your room."

Wren dropped her hand to her side and finally nodded.

9

THE FIGHT

On Sunday Wren wanted to push past Philip and Neil through the door to the Sunday School wing, but instead she meekly followed them. During the week it was Jordan Christian Academy, but on Sundays it was the church. She looked around for Tim, but didn't see his bright red hair. Sometimes he was late to Sunday School because he had to wake himself up and get himself ready, then ride his bike. Sometimes he was so early that he was first in the classroom. But today when she desperately needed to talk to him, Wren couldn't find him.

Bess motioned to Wren and patted the empty chair beside her. When Wren reached her side, she whispered, "Did you see who came today?"

"No. Who?" Wren shot a look around the crowded room.

"Paula Gantz." Bess made a face. "And her parents! They've never been here before, but maybe they thought they should come since Paula's enrolled in JCA."

Wren looked again for Tim's bright red head. "Did you see Tim yet?"

Bess frowned. "Tim? Who cares about Tim?" I thought you'd be angry about Paula coming. I thought you'd want Paula to stay away from here."

"I don't care about Paula right now! I need to talk to Tim."

Bess stuck out her bottom lip in a pout. "I think Tim's your best friend now instead of me."

"That's not so!"

"Then why are you looking for him now instead of talking to me?" Bess smoothed the soft arm of her sweater.

"Because." Wren craned her neck and looked around again. The Sunday School room was almost full. She rubbed her skirt over her legs and sighed heavily. "We didn't find Amos Pike yesterday."

Bess frowned and folded her arms over her chest. Her pink sweater matched her cheeks. Not a hair of her blonde head was out of place. "I think you're making up the whole mystery just like you did about Miss Brewster."

"I am not!" Boys and girls glanced at her and she sank lower in her seat and snapped her mouth closed.

Bess looked straight ahead. "If you weren't my best friend, I'd move away from you and make you sit all alone."

Wren jabbed her with her elbow. "Go ahead and sit somewhere else. See if I care. Sit with Paula Gantz!"

"I think I will!"

"Go right ahead! You're too dumb anyway."

"You're stupid." Bess gripped her small purse and her Bible. "You're so dumb that you see a mystery when there isn't one to see."

Wren's face flamed. "You're so dumb that you can't see that Neil doesn't even know you're alive!"

With a sob Bess jumped up and slipped across the room, sinking into a chair beside Paula.

Wren lifted her chin and tried to look as if she didn't care that Bess had walked away. Whispers buzzed around her and she pretended not to hear as the teacher, Carrie Cain, walked to the front of the class with her Bible.

Just then Tim dropped down beside Wren. "Thanks for saving me a place," he whispered.

"Time for class, boys and girls," Carrie called as she rapped on her desk.

Wren frowned at Tim, but didn't dare answer him. Carrie didn't allow talking in the class unless it was during the discussion.

Wren peeked over at Bess, but she was facing Carrie as if she didn't want to miss a single word she said. "Who cares if Bess is mad," she muttered under her breath, but her stomach tightened into a cold, hard ball that kept her from concentrating on the lesson.

After class Wren pulled Tim aside before his friends grabbed him. He smelled like syrup and pancakes. It made her hungry. "Dad wouldn't drive me around to look for Amos yesterday."

"That's too bad. I looked for awhile after you left, but I didn't find him." Tim scratched his neck and then his eye. "I didn't see Buster either."

Wren sighed heavily. She ignored Bess as she walked past with her nose in the air. "Will you look again today?"

Tim nodded. "Will you?"

"I'll try. I don't know if Mom will let me." Wren glanced around to make sure no one could hear her. Most of the others were already walking toward the sanctuary for morning worship. She leaned close to Tim. "I got yelled at for spying on Miss Brewster and Mr. Abram yesterday."

"That's too bad."

Wren gripped Tim's arm. "Look! There they are now!"

The teachers stood several feet away in deep conversation. Miss Brewster looked ready to cry. Mr. Abram looked angry. Wren and Tim walked toward them, then stopped a couple of feet away.

"How can you say that?" Mr. Abram asked gruffly.

"I mean it, too, Josh." Miss Brewster dabbed at her tears with a tissue. "I think we'd better get into church. I'm playing the piano when Jennifer sings."

"This isn't settled, Meg. We'll discuss this later."

"No, Josh! It is settled!" She walked away and Mr. Abram strode after her, his face dark with anger. Neither one had noticed Wren and Tim.

Triumphantly Wren turned to Tim. "See? There is a mystery! I knew it! I have the nose of a detective." She tapped her nose. "And I smell a mystery right there! She flung her arm out, her finger pointed dramatically.

Tim nodded, his eyes flashing with excitement. "I think you're right. But I think we'd better not spy on them again unless you want to be in worse trouble."

"I agree." Wren sighed heavily and touched the back of her hand to her forehead. "I'm just not appreciated. We'll have to find another way to learn the problem, then solve it." Wren walked to the sanctuary and sat toward the middle of the church, one pew ahead of her family. She knew she had to sit where they could see her so she'd know she wasn't in trouble. Tim sat beside her. Wren impatiently pushed aside the thought that Bess usually sat with her.

The orchestra played one of her favorite contemporary gospel songs and she listened to it, trying to forget about everything for awhile. During the praise and worship service she sang with all her might, but for once the words didn't seem to mean anything to her. When the offering plate was passed, she dropped in her money and waited for the feeling of gladness that always brought, but all she felt was a great emptiness inside.

Miss Brewster played the piano while Jennifer Anderson sang, filling the auditorium with the beautiful melody and words. Wren sat like a stone.

Tim nudged her and whispered, "What's wrong?"

She shrugged and pressed her lips into a thin, tight line. The fight with Bess played again in her mind. She linked her icy fingers together in her lap and opened her eyes wide to keep tears back.

Why should she feel bad about fighting with Bess? It was Bess's fault.

Wren settled back and tried to listen to the pastor, but his words couldn't push through the terrible darkness she felt inside.

Someone sneezed and someone else dropped a book. Wren glanced sideways only to find that Bess was sitting just across the aisle. Bess looked over at her before Wren looked away. Bess looked ready to cry. Wren quickly looked away and pretended to listen to the minister.

Wren bit her bottom lip. Why had she said anything to Bess about Neil? Why had she told Bess she was dumb? She knew Jesus wanted her to be kind and loving and not fight. Jesus wanted her to forgive Bess for saying bad things to her. Could she do it?

She glanced again at Bess. Bess was looking at her. A giant tear rolled down Bess's pale cheek. A giant tear welled up in Wren's eye and spilled out. She turned her head and wiped it away with the back of her hand before anyone else saw it.

Tim whispered something to her, but she didn't hear

and he didn't repeat it. Someone behind her rustled pages in a book.

During the closing prayer she stood with her hands locked over the back of the pew in front of her. She had to tell Bess she was sorry before Bess left the church or she wouldn't see her again until tomorrow morning. Bess and her family were going to spend the day in the country with her grandparents. Wren swallowed hard. She couldn't go a whole day and night without telling Bess she was sorry.

After the prayer, Tim said, "I'll call you after dinner and see if we can look for Amos."

She nodded, barely hearing him while she waited for a clear path out of her pew.

"What's wrong, Wren?" asked Tim, his voice low with concern.

She blinked hard to keep back tears. "I have to talk to Bess."

"Why?"

"I just do!" She wanted to leap over the pews to get to the aisle. Just then the people in her row moved and she saw Bess take a step toward her, then wait as if she was afraid to take another step.

Wren turned to Tim and half-smiled. "I'll talk to you later, Tim."

He nodded.

She walked toward Bess, stopped, squared her shoulders and lifted her chin high. Jesus would help her tell Bess she was sorry for being mean. Jesus would help her forgive Bess for being mean to her.

Four steps later she stood in front of Bess. "Hi," she said just above a whisper.

"Hi," said Bess, twisting the cuff on her sweater.

Wren took a deep breath, then blurted out, "I'm sorry for saying bad things to you, Bess."

Bess sniffed and blinked away fresh tears. "Me, too, Wren. Please forgive me."

"I do."

"Me, too."

Wren smiled and Bess smiled. "Friends again," they said together.

"You're my best friend and I never want to fight again," said Bess.

Wren wanted to hug Bess, but she only nodded. "Best friends again," she said.

10

THE DESERTED HOUSE

Tim and Wren stopped their bikes in the shade of a tall oak.

Tim rubbed a piece of dirt off his bike frame, then looked up at Wren with a serious look on his freckled face. "We'll find Amos today."

She walked her bike closer to him, her dark eyes wide. "You sound very sure. Did you see Buster again?"

"No, but we prayed and I think we should believe that God will answer."

Wren nodded. "You're right, Tim." She glanced around. "Where shall we look first?"

"Simple deduction, Wren. I checked to see if he was home and found Stella still there with a story that Amos was spending Sunday with a friend."

Wren's eyes flashed. "What a lie!"

"I wanted to yell at her, but I walked away as if it didn't matter to me." Tim gripped his handlebars tighter. "Stella makes me so mad!"

"Me, too." She could think of all kinds of mean things to say and do to Stella, but she knew she couldn't do any of them. "Where do we go next?"

Tim waved his arm. "We start where you saw Buster yesterday."

"Great idea! It's not far from here."

"We'll go from house to house if necessary."

Wren nodded. "Dad says there's a lot of footwork in detective work. Let's go."

"We'll stay together this time."

"And we'll start on Green Street, go down Maple, across Parker and up Elm back to Green. Dad calls that being systematic."

"Systematic. That's a good word."

"I like to hear detective talk. It makes me feel like a detective." She remember that her dad had said she was not a detective and her face fell.

"What's wrong?" Tim peered closely at her.

She took a deep, steadying breath. "Do you think I'm a detective?"

"Sure. Do you think I am?"

She hadn't given it a lot of thought. She knew that he wanted to be one and that he was good at solving mysteries. Finally she nodded.d "You couldn't have your own agency yet, but to me you're already a detective."

His thin chest swelled with pride and he rubbed back his red hair. "Some day I'll have my own agency. Maybe you and I can be partners."

"Maybe." Last year she'd have turned him down, but now that they were friends it sounded like a good idea. Together they could conquer the world.

He grinned and she smiled back.

"We'd better go." Wren led the way and they rode from house to house. They took turns knocking and asking about Amos. Some people were home and some weren't. Some were nice, but others snapped and snarled for being disturbed on a Sunday afternoon. No one had seen Amos and some didn't know him. On Elm Street Wren rode up to a deserted house with Tim directly behind her.

Wren looked at the two story weathered house and wrinkled her pert nose. Boards covered the windows. A shutter on an upstairs window hung loose. Weeds grew among the shrubs and the hedge along the side of the porch looked as if it hadn't been trimmed for years. "It looks like a haunted house," she said with a shiver.

Tim left his bike on the overgrown lawn and ran up the steps. "It would be a good place for Amos to hide."

Wren ran to the door and knocked. Paint peeled off on her knuckles.

Tim rattled the knob, but it wouldn't turn.

Just then Buster poked his head around the porch and barked three short barks.

"Buster!" Wren ran toward him, and he barked and

zipped around the corner of the house.

"Don't scare him!" called Tim, running after Wren.

Abruptly Wren stopped and Tim crashed into her, sending them both sprawling to the ground. Wren jumped up and rubbed her hands on her jeans. "Where'd he go?" She looked around frantically. Suddenly she spotted Buster a few feet away behind a shrub, eyeing them suspiciously, his small black ears high. "There he is!" she cried.

"It's us, Buster," said Tim, moving forward and holding out a hand.

"We're friends," said Wren. "Amos knows us and we're friends. Remember?"

Buster barked a short, sharp bark and didn't move. A twig stuck in his hair beside his left front leg.

Wren looked at Buster, then at the house with a thoughtful frown. "I wonder if Amos is hiding inside."

"I wonder if he is! If he is, why didn't he come when we called?"

"I don't know. Unless . . . "

"Unless what, Wren?"

She wiped a hand across her face. "Unless he's . . . he's hurt." She walked around the house with Tim beside her. Tim tried the back door but it was locked. They walked around the two story house looking for broken windows, but all the windows were boarded up.

As they peeked behind the bushes against the house,

Wren suddenly pointed at a small opening behind an evergreen. "Look, Tim!" She peered inside to find only darkness. It smelled old and dusty.

Tim dropped beside her. "Looks like this board used to cover it."

"Amos," Wren called. Her voice sounded hollow. "Amos!"

Tim reached inside. "It's like a slide. I'll slide down it and you stay out here in case I can't find a way out."

She pushed him away. "Let me slide inside. I'm smaller."

He frowned, then finally shrugged. "Maybe you better. I hate spiders and it looks like this basement would be full of them."

Wren shivered. "I wish we had a flashlight."

"I have one at my house. I'll ride home and get it and you look around." He dashed away toward his bike, then ran back. "Don't you dare get into trouble."

"Me?" she asked innocently.

"I mean it, Wren. Don't try anything on your own."

"Just get the flashlight, Tim."

He sighed heavily and ran to his bike.

Wren knelt in front of the opening. The bush scratched her shoulders. "Amos, are you in there?" She listened but all she heard was a car passing on the street and her own heartbeat.

Just then Buster rubbed against her arm. She smiled and carefully touched his head.

"Do you remember me now, Buster? I won't hurt you and I won't hurt Amos. I wish you could talk so you could tell me where he is. You know where he is, don't you?"

Buster whined and wriggled. "Is he inside hiding from Stella?"

Buster licked Wren's face with his small, wet tongue. She giggled and wiped the moisture off.

She stuck her head inside the hole. "Amos! Are you in there? It's me, Wren House. Buster's with me." She listened carefully. Had she heard a muffled sound? "Amos?" She listened again. Her heart leaped. There was a sound from inside! Where was Tim with the flashlight?

Suddenly Buster dived through the opening and slid out of sight.

"Buster!" Wren leaned in as far as she could go. She touched the cold piece of steel. Butterflies fluttered in her stomach as an idea popped into her head. Before she could change her mind she slid inside headfirst with her arms outstretched. She slipped down, down into the darkness, then struck the floor. She managed to stop her fall before her head crashed into the concrete floor.

Buster met her there and licked her cheek. She pulled herself together and kept her hand on his head. Slowly she stood and a cobweb brushed her cheek. She cried out and Buster barked. The sounds echoed around the room.

"What have I done, Buster?" she whispered through a tight throat.

He pulled away from her and she heard him running across the room, sniffing as he went. She shivered and looked around helplessly. "I wish I could see in the dark." The small opening high above was the only light. Dust tickled her nose and she sneezed.

"Buster, come back!" She stepped forward, holding her hands out for protection and to feel. "Amos?" Are you in here?"

A low moan reached her and she shivered. "Amos?"

What if Amos wasn't there? What if a stranger leaped out and killed her? She spun around and headed back toward the dim light. She tripped and sprawled to the floor. Something small and furry ran over her hand and she screamed.

11

THE RESCUE

Wren jumped up and rubbed her hand hard to brush off the feeling of the mouse. Her heart raced and shivers ran up and down her spine. With trembling hands she tucked her hair behind her ears.

"Buster?" Her voice cracked. "Buster, where are you?" There was no answering bark or wriggling body.

Slowly she walked to the slide and gripped the sides to walk up it to freedom. Just as she reached the top, she slipped and fell back down the chute. She landed with a thud at the bottom. "Ouch!"

Carefully she walked back up the chute, gripping the sides so hard her knuckles ached. Just before she reached the top she heard a sound behind her. Her stomach tightened. She stopped and listened, her head turned, her mouth bone dry.

"Wren," a weak, low voice called.

She gasped. Had she heard right?

"Wren, help me." The voice was stronger this time and

it came from the room in back of her.

Carefully she slid back to the floor. "Amos? Is that you?"

"Yes. I'm . . . hurt."

"Where are you?"

"Here. In a room next to where you are."

Just then from outdoors she heard, "Wren! Wren House, where did you go?" It was Tim and he sounded angry and impatient.

She scrambled part way up the chute. "Tim! Down here! Bring the light here."

A light flashed in her eyes and she blinked.

"Watch out, Wren."

"Wait! Stay there and hand me the light."

"Move, Wren! I'm coming down." Tim sat on the chute and Wren leaped out of the way just as he slipped down. The light bobbed wildly, catching wooden beams and black cobwebs in its glow.

"I'm so glad to see you! Amos is down here!" Wren grabbed Tim's arm and tugged. "Shine the light around and let's find a door. He said he's in a room next to this one."

"I thought you said you'd stay outdoors."

"I thought I would."

"I knew you wouldn't." He sounded angry and she touched his arm.

"Buster jumped down and I had to follow him. Didn't I?"

"I guess so." Tim shone the light around the empty basement. A huge furnace stood several feet away with thick arms reaching out from it across the ceiling. Cobwebs hung low. "It's dirty down here."

"There are mice, too." She shivered and made a face. Just then the light caught the doorway, and bobbed away. "Hold it!" Wren said. She tugged Tim's arm until the light once again shone on the doorway. "That's it!"

"I see it!" Tim said excitedly and led the way. Wren hung onto the back of his shirt. A mouse scurried out of the way and Wren shrieked. The light beam caught Buster's eyes inside the room. They gleamed brightly. He barked and then growled.

"It's all right, boy," said Amos in a weak voice. "They're friends. Thank God!"

"Amos!" Wren dashed around Tim and dropped beside the man lying in a heap on the damp floor. "Amos, what's wrong?"

Tim knelt on the other side of Amos. "Are you hurt?"

Amos groaned and tried to move. "Yes. My leg. I can't walk."

Buster pushed his nose against Amos and whined.

"Can you walk if we help you?" Wren tugged on Amos's arm.

"I can try." He hoisted himself up, then fell back. "I can't. It may be broken."

"How'd you get down here?" asked Tim.

"Down the coal chute, same as you." Amos scooted back and leaned against the wall. "I had to find a place to stay for the night and I slid down here. Buster followed me." His voice grew stronger. "I slept upstairs and when I started down here yesterday morning, I tripped on the steps and fell."

"Oh, Amos!" cried Wren. She pressed her cheek against his arm. His shirt felt smooth, but smelled of perspiration and dirt.

"I knew you two would find me." He patted Wren's and Tim's hands. "I prayed that God would send you."

"We prayed we'd find you," said Wren.

Amos sniffed and rubbed a rough hand over his nose. "I sent Buster to find you, too."

"He did," said Tim. "We followed him here."

"But now we have to get you out of here, Amos," said Wren. "Try to stand again. Lean on me more. I'm stronger than I look."

Amos struggled to stand with Tim on one side and Wren on the other. His hand pushed Wren down, down until her knees buckled. She dropped to the floor. "It's no use," Amos said with a groan, sinking down also.

"We'll have to go get help," said Wren, rubbing her shoulder and her knees.

"Who?" asked Tim. He didn't have anyone he could ask.

Wren moved restlessly. "I could get Dad."

"I guess you'd better," said Amos.

Wren tucked her hair behind her ears. Would Dad believe her and help? "Tim, walk me to the window with your light. I'll climb out and call Dad. Maybe Mrs. Thomkins will let me use her phone." She touched the old man's cheek. "I'll be back soon. I promise."

"I know you will," he said with a catch in his voice. "I trust you both."

A few minutes later she was on her bike, pedaling fast toward Mina Thomkins's house. Hopefully Mrs. Thomkins would let her use her phone, and hopefully Dad would come without an argument.

At the yellow house she knocked on the back door. She held her breath and waited. After a long time the door opened a crack and Mina Thomkins peered out.

"What do you want? I don't want to buy anything."

Wren smiled and moved a little closer to Mrs. Thomkins. "Remember me, Mrs. Thomkins? I'm Wren. My friend Tim and I talked to you Saturday."

"Oh, yes!" Mrs. Thomkins opened the door wider. "You're filthy! What happened to you?"

A black streak ran from her right temple to the corner of her mouth, and cobwebs clung to her hair. Her sweater and jeans were dirty and her once white tennis shoes were scuffed and dirty.

"I fell in a basement. I found my friend Amos but he's hurt and I need to call my dad to come help. Could I use

99

your phone to call him? Please?"

Mrs. Thomkins nodded and stepped aside for Wren to enter. "The phone's in the kitchen."

"Thanks." The kitchen looked clean and tidy with an old fashioned oak table and three cane bottomed chairs pushed up to it. Wren reached for the white phone on the counter beside several potted plants. She wrinkled her nose at the sight of her hands.

A few seconds later Wren heard her dad's voice on the other end. She gripped the phone tighter and forced back a shiver. As quickly as she could she told him what had happened, her voice strong even though she felt like whimpering like a baby. "Could you come right now, Dad?"

He was quiet for what seemed a long time. "I'll be right there, Wren."

"I'll wait outside the house for you. And, Dad . . . thanks!" She hung up and turned to Mrs. Thomkins. "He'll help."

"Good. I wish I could."

"You did. Thanks for letting me use the phone."

"Is Amos hurt very badly?"

"I don't know, but he can't walk."

"Maybe I should get my coat and go with you."

Wren shook her head. "You don't have to, but thanks anyway. There really isn't anything you can do."

Mrs. Thomkins folded her thin arms over her chest and looked very concerned. "If I can help at all, let me know."

"I will. And I'll call to tell you how Amos is after we get home."

Mrs. Thomkins let Wren out the door and Wren rode back to the deserted house, her face red from excitement as well as the warm wind whipping against her.

"Tim!" She stuck her head in the opening. "Tim, I'm back. Dad will be here soon."

A light bobbed across the darkness and Tim stopped at the bottom of the chute. "I'll see if I can unlock a door to let your dad inside. I tried a while ago, but couldn't. Amos gave me another suggestion, so I'll try it."

"How is Amos?"

"He's all right, but he needs something to eat and drink right away. I gave him a sourball that I had in my pocket to suck on." He didn't tell her that he'd sucked it awhile himself, then stuck it in his pocket to collect lint and bits of dirt. He'd cleaned it off the best he could for Amos. "His leg feels better, he says."

"Good. I'll run around to the sidewalk to wait for Dad. Call me if you get a door open."

She waited, jumping from one foot to the other. Every car that drove past sent tingles along her spine. Would Dad scold her for daring to go inside the deserted house?

Finally her dad drove up in the station wagon. He jumped out and ran to join Wren. He wore jeans and a green sweatshirt. His dark hair was mussed. He caught Wren's hand in a firm hold and smiled reassuringly down at her. "Show me where he is."

Just then the front door popped open and Tim stood there looking dirty, but triumphant. "I got it open!"

Wren led Dad to the basement. Several minutes later they helped Amos up the steps and out of the house into the station wagon. Buster followed close behind, sniffing Sam House's ankle.

"The leg doesn't seem to be broken," said Wren's dad as he eased Amos into the back seat. "But I called Dr. Gantz before I left home and asked if he'd check it for us."

Amos shook his head. His dirty face was covered with new whiskers and he looked as if he hadn't slept for a long time. "I don't have money for a doctor."

"Dr. Gantz is our neighbor," said Wren.

"He won't charge you," said Sam. He turned to Tim. "Stick your bike in the back with Wren's and ride home with us. I know you'll want to know the outcome. And I want to know more details about this strange story." He looked right at Wren, and she met his look squarely.

12

MOM'S HELP

Trembling, Wren walked into her mother's study. One entire wall was covered with books that her mom had had to study. Plants hung at the row of windows at the side of the big desk. Wren took a deep breath. "Dad said you wanted to see me as soon as I showered and changed clothes, Mom."

Lorrene walked from around her desk, a slight smile on her pretty face. "Did Dad take Amos to clean up and change?"

Wren nodded.

"Good." Lorrene stood in the middle of the room that she'd decorated herself last year to look homey, yet professional. "Sit down, Wren."

Wren sank to the edge of the leather sofa. "Are you mad at me, Mom?"

"Wren, no! Please, don't think that." Lorrene sat across from Wren in a soft blue chair. "This is rather hard for me, Wren."

"What?" Nothing ever seemed too hard for Mom.

Lorrene House took a deep breath and wrapped her hands around her jean clad knees. "Wren, I was wrong. I was wrong about you and your whole involvement with Amos Pike. I wanted you to drop it because I didn't want one more mystery of yours to embarrass me. I was wrong. And I am very sorry."

"It's all right, Mom. Sometimes I am wrong."

Lorrene rolled her eyes. "Sometimes? Often! But Amos could've died alone down in that basement if you hadn't persevered. I'm glad you kept looking for Amos until you found him."

"Me, too."

Lorrene slipped across to the couch beside Wren and put her arm around her. Wren liked the smell of her perfume and the feel of her arm around her. Sometimes Mom was too busy to find time for her. "You have a sharp mind, Wren, and I am glad you use it. You're a caring person, and I'm glad of that."

Wren felt warm and soft inside. She smiled.

Lorrene rubbed her cheek against Wren's head. "Wren Lorrene House, I am proud of you."

Wren's eyes widened. "You are?"

"I am proud of you as a person and proud that you're my daughter."

"Even if I do detective work?"

"Even then." Her mom kissed Wren's flushed cheeks and hugged her close.

"I love you, Mom."

"And I love you."

Wren hugged Mom as tight as she could, then pulled away just far enough to look into her face. "We have to help Amos, Mom."

"Yes. Yes, Wren, we do. I'll do everything I can."

"Oh, Mom! Thank you!" Wren hugged her again with her face pressed into her mom's neck.

A few minutes later Tim knocked on the open door. "Mr. House says to come to the living room for a meeting.

"Wren jumped up and followed Tim. "Where's Buster?"

"On the back porch waiting for Amos."

"That's good. Mom doesn't like dogs in the house."

"Mine won't let any animals in our house, either."

Wren stepped into the living room. She smiled at Amos and sat on the couch beside him. "Do you feel better now, Amos?"

"Much better." He rubbed his damp hair back. "But I'll feel even better when I'm back in my own place."

"We'll see that you get back there," said Wren's dad.

"Stella must be worried about you," said Wren. "I would worry about my brothers if they didn't have a place to live."

"She's not worried about me," said Amos. "She doesn't care a fig about me."

"This is ridiculous!" Lorrene jumped up from the

rocker and paced the living room floor while Wren, Amos, Tim and Sam watched her. "No one takes over a house like that!" She stopped right in front of Amos. He pulled into himself and Wren slid closer to him. He seemed helpless with his sprained and now splinted ankle. "Your own sister!" Lorrene flung out her arms and looked from one to the other. "This is really ridiculous!"

"But it's true," said Tim in a small voice.

"It is, Mom," whispered Wren.

"It is," said Sam, pushing himself up from his armchair. He took Lorrene's arm and sat her down in his chair, then perched on the arm. "Now that that is settled once again, let's see what we can do to help Amos."

"I won't go to the police," said Amos.

Wren rested her head on Amos's arm. He'd taken a shower and now wore clean clothes that belonged to Dad. He'd also eaten a bowl of chicken soup and drunk a tall glass of cold milk. Dr. Gantz had strapped his ankle and said to walk on crutches for a few days. Amos also had a huge bruise on his thigh from hitting the stairs when he'd fallen. Dr. Gantz had said that Amos was all right, but needed to rest after such an ordeal. Mom has said that he could stay with them and sleep in Philip's room. Philip would stay in Neil's room until Amos left. Wren knew Philip didn't mind. It gave him a better chance to learn more about Neil's computer. Neil didn't mind either. It gave him a chance to show off to Philip how smart he was.

"The law is on your side." Lorrene shook her finger at Amos.

"No police," said Amos stubbornly.

"It's his own sister," said Tim.

"She knows I won't go to the police," said Amos. "That's why she feels secure now that she's inside."

"We'll have to get her out," said Sam. "And get you back inside."

"And, we'll have to find a way to keep her from doing this again," said Lorrene.

Wren leaped up, her cheeks flushed and her eyes sparkling. "I know!"

"What?" asked everyone at once.

"We'll trick her into leaving. We'll think of a brilliant plan that will make her leave the house long enough for Amos to get back inside."

"What's the brilliant plan?" asked Tim.

Lorrene's face lit up. "I know!"

Wren's mouth dropped open. "You do? What?"

"That's my sweetheart," said Sam, hugging his wife.

Wren turned to Amos. "My mom's really smart."

Amos moved restlessly. "I'm willing to try it, whatever it is."

"What is it, Mom?" asked Wren, barely able to sit still.

Lorrene jumped up and stood near the piano that she played once in a while. She tugged her sweater down over her jeans and smiled smugly. "Here's what we'll do." In a few words Lorrene outlined her plan and Amos added a suggestion.

Wren puffed out with pride. "It's perfect, Mom. Isn't it, Amos?"

He nodded.

"Will it work?" asked Tim.

"It will," said Amos. "I know my sister."

"When do we do it?" asked Sam, rubbing his hands together.

"Not tonight," said Lorrene. "Amos, you really need a quiet night with us." She made a face, then laughed. "If there is such a thing in this house. No, we won't do it tonight, but tomorrow."

"Tomorrow I'll be back in my own place," said Amos with a sigh. "Me and Buster together." He blinked moisture from his eyes. "I don't know how I'll ever thank you. I have friends after all."

"Friends!" Wren jumped up. "I forgot! I told Mrs. Thomkins that I'd call her to let her know that Amos is all right. She's your friend, too, Amos."

"I haven't spoken to her since my wife passed on. I'll have to make sure I call her once I'm home again."

"Well, I have to get home," said Tim, pushing himself up. "I'll be over after school tomorrow to help."

"Meet us at Amos's house," said Wren.

Tim nodded, and walked out while Wren stopped in the kitchen to use the phone. The smell of chicken soup still hung in the cheery room. A dirty bowl and glass sat on the counter beside the sink. She thought about Amos as she dialed the phone.

"Mrs. Thomkins, this is Wren House. Amos is here with us. He's O.K."

"I'm glad to hear that."

"Did your grandson mow your lawn yet?"

"No. He didn't. I don't know what became of that boy."

Wren's face lit up. Was it another mystery? "Did you call him?"

"I tried, but I didn't get an answer."

"Tim and I will mow your lawn tomorrow if your grandson doesn't get there before. First we have to take Amos home. He's staying with us tonight and tomorrow afternoon he'll go home."

"Don't concern yourself over my lawn."

"We said we'd mow it, and we will." Maybe she could get Philip and Neil to help. "See you tomorrow, Mrs. Thomkins."

"I don't know what to say, dear." She sounded as if she was crying."

"We want to help. See you tomorrow about five o'clock."

Wren turned from the phone to find Mom watching her from the doorway. The look on Mom's face made Wren's heart leap.

"Wren, you are a wonderful little girl. I am so proud of you!"

Wren ran across the room and flung her arms around Mom's waist.

13

THE BRILLIANT PLAN

Wren stood with Amos on the far side of the garage and peeked around the corner at Amos's house. She could see Stella watering a plant at the window. "She thinks she gets to stay here," whispered Wren.

"She does look sure of herself," said Amos, leaning heavily on his crutches. "What time is it?" Buster brushed against his leg.

Wren looked at the watch her Grandma had given her for Christmas last year. "It's almost four-thirty. Tim, dad and mom should be here any minute." Wren grinned and pressed her hand to her racing heart. It would be fun to watch her parents in action.

Just then she saw Tim riding down the street from one end. Her mom was right behind him in her car. Then, she saw her dad driving toward them in the station wagon. She knew Tim was supposed to swerve in front of the car and her dad would screech to a halt. Tim was going to ride to the curb and fall into the grass. That would draw

Stella out even if Wren's mom had to go to the door to ask for help and for Stella to be a witness.

Suddenly, Amos and Wren saw the screen door open and Stella look out cautiously. Wrapping her sweater around her, Stella moved down the steps to the mailbox by the street.

Unexpectedly, Wren saw Tim swerve—but not in the direction planned. Instead he headed toward Stella. Riding fast, he cut in behind her to see what he was doing, Wren ran out of hiding and joined him on the sidewalk. They had cut her off from the house! Amos quickly joined them and together they faced a stunned Stella.

On the street, Wren's mom and dad slowed to a stop and jumped out of their cars. Rushing up the sidewalk, they joined the other three and surrounded Stella.

"Amos!" Stella cried. "W- What's happening? What are you doing?" Stella tried to break out of the circle, but Sam stopped her with a gentle hand on her arm.

"You've lost, Stella," he said firmly.

She jerked free and rubbed her arm. "What have you done to me?"

"My friends have helped me to get my house again," said Amos.

"No!" cried Stella, shaking her head. "No! No! No!"

Amos walked toward the porch and the others followed. "Let's sit out here and talk, Stella. With my friends here, I don't think I'll have any more trouble with you." Looking her squarely in the eye, he said, "This is my house and you can't take it over."

She stamped her foot. "It's my house!"

Lorrene walked to Stella, holding out her business card. "I'm a lawyer, Stella, and I know the law. This house belongs to your brother. You have no right to it."

Stella seemed to shrink into herself and suddenly looked ten years older. "But I have no place to go," she whispered desperately.

"You have your apartment," said Amos.

"No, I don't. They raised the rent and I can't pay it. I don't have anywhere to live." Stella dabbed away a tear.

Wren felt a stirring of sympathy for Stella.

Amos leaned against his crutches. "You can't live with me. I only have one bedroom. Besides, you hate Buster and you hate me."

Stella poked out her chin. "And you hate me!"

"I think there's been enough talk about hating," said Lorrene firmly. She gripped Stella's arm and sat down beside her on the porch. "You two are brother and sister. Family. How can you hate each other?"

Amos snapped his mouth closed. Stella turned her back on Amos. She sank back against a front porch post and burst into tears, sobbing into her hands.

"I've lost everything. First, my son. Then my husband. Now, my home. There's nothing left."

"Your son?" Wren asked in surprise. "I didn't know you

had a child."

"It was a long time ago," Stella sobbed. "He was killed when he rode his bike in front of a car."

Lorrene's eyes widened in dismay as she looked first at her husband and then at Amos.

Amos hung his head.

"Amos," Lorrene asked numbly, "did you know about this when we made our plan?" Amos refused to meet Lorrene's eyes. He just nodded.

"How could you let us plan to deceive your sister that way?" asked Sam.

"What way?" asked Stella.

Holding Stella's hand, Lorrene explained their idea and how it had been unnecessary when they had spotted her in the yard. Tim had acted quickly, on his own, and had solved the situation through his quick thinking.

Her eyes wide in fright, Stella gasped, "But it was so dangerous! Anything could have happened. Tim could have been hurt!"

Wren and Tim looked at each other. It had only seemed like an adventure to them.

"Amos, you knew!" Stella cried in anguish. "How could you?"

Amos hung his head. Sorrow filled his eyes as he finally looked up at Stella and the others. "Yes, I knew. I even suggested that part of the plan. I didn't mean to hurt you, Stella, but I knew it would get you out of the house. I'm sorry." He hung his head again.

"And we certainly didn't want to hurt Tim!" exclaimed Wren. "We just wanted to get you out of the house so our friend Amos could get back in."

Amos took a deep breath and looked at Stella. "I'm sorry, Stella. I shouldn't have. I was wrong."

Lorrene House spoke up. "We were all wrong, Stella. Sometimes the Lord has to let us go our own way, before we give up and ask Him to help us. We should never have planned to trick you. We're sorry and ask that you forgive us. The Lord worked it all out better than we could have anyway."

Stella looked amazed at the genuine sorrow she could see in the faces of Sam and Lorrene House.

Wren knelt beside Stella. "Don't cry anymore. We'll help you find a place to live."

Stella lifted her haggard face. "I don't have enough money."

"Maybe you could rent a room from someone," said Wren, thinking about Mina Thomkins and her offer to help.

Stella shook her head. "I looked around for rooms to rent and I don't have that kind of money."

Amos cleared his throat. "I could pay part of your rent each month."

"Why would you do that?" Stella stared at him in surprise.

"You're my sister."

"You don't care about me."

"I don't want you starving or freezing this winter."

Stella stood up with Sam's helping hand. "Amos . . . thank you. I will take your help and I won't try to take your house away from you."

Wren ran to the door. "Amos, may I use your phone?"

He nodded and held the door wide for her before following her inside.

"Who're you going to call?" asked her mom.

"Mina Thomkins," said Wren.

"Great idea," said Tim, smiling.

Wren dialed Mina Thomkins and told her what had happened. "Do you think Stella could rent a room from you until she can find something that she can afford?"

Mina Thomkins was silent for awhile. "Bring her over and I'll talk with her."

"Thank you!" Wren looked up at Amos. "She agreed."

"Good." Amos hobbled to the door to tell the others.

Wren spoke into the receiver again. "Did your grandson mow your lawn yet?"

"Yes, this morning, and it looks beautiful again."

Wren felt disappointed. She wanted another mystery to solve. "Good. We'll bring Stella right over."

Several minutes later Stella sat in Lorrene's car with her things piled in the trunk. Wren and Tim rode their bikes and they all met at the yellow house.

"Amos is happy and Stella has a home now," said Wren.

"Just in time for the movie at school Wednesday," said Tim.

"Maybe Mrs. Thomkins and Stella will want to go see the movie of Amos Pike."

"Maybe," said Tim.

Wren ran to the house to ask.

14

MOVIE DAY

Wren rubbed her cotton skirt down over her legs and tried to settle the butterflies in her stomach. Bess sat on one side of her in a pink ruffled dress, and Sandra Connors sat on the other side. Wren closed her eyes and took a deep breath. Soon it would be her turn to sing. She peeked around the room and found her family sitting with Amos, Stella, and Mrs. Thomkins. Amos looked happy. Stella looked as if she was enjoying the program, but feeling a little strange among strangers. Mrs. Thomkins smiled at everyone. Other parents and friends filled the auditorium. The smell of coffee drifted in from the cafeteria where they would serve cookies, coffee and punch after the program.

Nathan Bronski finished his flute solo with his eyebrows almost touching his hair, and sat down beside Tim while everyone clapped. Sometimes Wren thought Nathan's eyebrows would pop right off his head when he hit a high note.

Miss Brewster walked to the front of the room. She looked very pretty in her navy blue skirt and jacket with a red and white blouse, but there was a great sadness in her eyes that worried Wren. "I'd like to take time right now to give special thanks to Sam House for helping us develop the pictures we have around the room. Mr. House, thank you. We appreciate it. You did a marvelous job."

Sam smiled and nodded as applause filled the room. Lorrene patted Sam's arm and smiled at him. Wren wanted to leap up and shout, "That's my dad!" But she clapped along with everyone. She remembered the great disaster with Miss Brewster and wrinkled her nose. Mom was right. She did find mysteries even when there were none. After this, she'd have to make very sure she didn't try to solve something that didn't need solving.

Miss Brewster announced the first movie. Jason Nichols dimmed the lights and the movie started on the big screen TV that they used. It showed several boys washing cars, collecting money, and giving the money away to help feed the poor. Part of the movie was clear, but part was blurry. Nobody seemed to mind.

Finally it was Wren's turn to sing. Mom had bought her a new orange skirt and lighter orange sweater with short sleeves to wear. She knew she looked nice. Her hair was brushed until it shone. She stood in front of the crowd with her hands at her sides. She smiled right at her family and they smiled back. Dad winked at her just as

Miss Stevens hit the first note on the piano. Wren opened her mouth and the beautiful melody of Messiah filled the room. She sang the words from her heart, sang to her family, sang in praise to God, and sang to Amos Pike and Mrs. Thomkins, her new friends, and even to Stella.

When she finished the last glorious note, applause broke out and didn't stop until she bowed twice, then sat down. Mrs. Brewster stood.

Bess leaned close and whispered, "That was perfect, Wren."

"Thanks." Wren locked her hands in her lap and sat very still. She was glad that God had given her the special gift of singing. She loved to sing, but she was always happy when she was finished.

The program continued until finally it was time for the last movie, the movie that Wren, Bess and Tim had made.

"Here it is," whispered Wren when the lights were dimmed. New butterflies fluttered in her stomach. What would everyone think of the movie? Bess and Tim were as pleased with it as she was. But now everyone would see it and the truth would come out. Maybe it would look as amateurish as Paula's had. Wren squirmed and rubbed her icy hands together. Sometimes it was easy to think that her work was really great, only to learn that it really wasn't.

She glanced back at Tim to find him looking at her as if he wanted to run and she knew he had the same doubts.

Tim had filmed the opening of the movie showing old

Mrs. Black making an apple pie with Bess helping. While the pie baked Mrs. Black and Bess cleaned up the mess and talked. Tim had flashed the camera to the oven and back to Mrs. Black working. Finally Mrs. Black pulled the pie out of the oven with steam rising from the fork pricks in the top crust.

The audience oohed and aahed and Wren laughed with Bess. The first time Wren had seen it, it had made her hungry.

The next scene showed Mrs. Black and Bess giving the pie away to a young mother busy with four children, two still in diapers. The young mother hugged Mrs. Black and Bess and the children waved as they left.

Wren sank lower in her seat as Mr. Caulder and Tim came on the screen, mowing a lawn. Wren had taken this segment. She could tell each time her hand had jerked with the camera, and she wanted to sink out of sight.

Bess nudged her and giggled when the camera bobbed around to show only Tim's feet, then the top of his head and finally his hands on the mower.

On the screen Tim and Mr. Caulder walked down the street with the mower to another lawn to show that they were helping others with yard work.

The next segment showed Mrs. Sinder telling a Bible story to a yard full of children. Bess had taken it and had tried very hard to get close ups of everyone. Once she moved so close to Mrs. Sinder that she took only her mouth. Wren could see Mrs. Sinder's chipped tooth. The audience laughed and Bess groaned.

Next came Amos Pike and his dog Buster. Wren clapped and a few others joined in. All of her class knew that Amos was visiting today. He'd brought Buster, but Buster had refused to come inside. He was probably still waiting for Amos under the bush beside the school.

Amos showed off his marigolds, sat on the step and talked to Bess and Wren, helped the paper boy pick up the bundle of papers that he'd spilled out of his bag, then had Buster do all of his tricks. Everyone clapped as Buster jumped through Amos's arms. Wren swelled with pride. She didn't want the movie to end. She sighed as Jason brightened the lights while the audience clapped and cheered.

Miss Brewster slowly walked to the front and looked out at the crowd. Tears glistened in her eyes. She tried to speak and couldn't, then tried again.

Wide eyed, Wren sat up, suddenly as quiet as everyone around her. A funny feeling tightened her stomach. Why was Miss Brewster acting this way? What was wrong? Maybe it had something to do with the mystery.

"This movie touched me," said Miss Brewster. She cleared her throat. "I . . . I have been planning to leave JCA and move away."

Whispers rippled across the room. Wren shot a knowing look at Tim.

"My mother died last year and my dad is alone. I've felt badly about that and thought I should go live with him and take care of him." Miss Brewster dabbed at the corner of her eye with a tissue. "He told me that he has made a life for himself and that I should do the same for myself. But I didn't believe him. For some reason I thought that older people didn't know how to function happily when they were alone."

Wren glanced at Mr. Abram and saw the intent look on his face.

"After seeing this movie, I see that an older person can indeed have a productive, happy life." Miss Brewster smiled. "I don't have to leave here after all. I'm going to stay here and make a life for myself, and Dad will stay in his home and continue to live happily there. My class made their movies to show Christians in action. We wanted to show God's Word put to work in everyday life. The movie makers wanted to show people helping others." Miss Brewster beamed at her students. "Class you helped me, and I thank you."

Wren clapped along with everyone else. She noticed that Mr. Abram clapped the loudest and longest.

Later she stood with Bess and Tim to bow as the audience applauded their work.

Bess tucked a stray strand of blond hair in place and looked to see if Neil was clapping. He was and she glowed with happiness.

"Let's take Amos, Stella, and Mrs. Thomkins for coffee and cookies," said Wren. "We'll introduce them to everyone."

"Amos will have lots of friends now," said Tim.

Wren led the way through the crowd to Amos and the women.

"I'm a celebrity, thanks to you three," said Amos, grinning crookedly as they walked to the cafeteria. "I don't think I'm going to be lonely after this."

Stella took the coffee Wren handed her. Her round face was thoughtful. "I didn't know there were people around that helped other people. I'm glad I met all of you. I want to have those kind of friends so I can learn to help others."

"Good for you, Stella," said Amos.

"We're getting to be very good friends," said Mina Thomkins, smiling at Stella. "It's enjoyable having someone in my home again."

"I like it, too," said Stella. "I've been lonely."

"If you'd forget about our feud, we could be friends," said Amos.

Stella smiled and touched his arm. "I can forget it if you can."

He nodded. "I'll go so far as to invite you to dinner Sunday if you'll come."

Stella blinked away tears. "I'll come."

"So will I," said Mrs. Thomkins. "I'll even bake an

apple pie."

"I'll help," said Stella with a chuckle.

Just then Wren noticed Mr. Abram motion to Miss Brewster. Wren glanced at Tim and Bess, but they were busy talking to friends. Wren hesitated, then slipped away from Amos and walked after Miss Brewster.

In the empty hall she saw Mr. Abram pull Miss Brewster close and kiss her. Wren smiled and took a step forward, then stopped. She wanted to stay and watch and listen, but she turned and slowly walked back to her family.

"Hi, Dad," Wren said, slipping her hand through his arm. "Did you like our movie?"

Sam bent his head and kissed his daughter's cheek. "It was great! Who knows? You might want to be a movie director or producer when you grow up."

"No way, Dad." Wren squared her shoulders and looked him right in the eye. "I'm going to be a detective just like you."

"I heard that," said Mom, tugging playfully on Wren's hair. "Maybe by the time you're grown up, I'll be used to the idea."

Wren hugged Mom, then Dad. Maybe they'd get used to her being a detective a whole lot sooner if she found another case to solve. She glanced around the room carefully.